MAHER AREF ABBAS, M.D.

BEYOND THE MAGIC SCALPEL

The Private Ordeals of Three Young Surgeons

SYTAC HEALTH PUBLISHING · USA

BEYOND THE MAGIC SCALPEL.
Copyright © 1997 by Maher Aref Abbas, M.D.
All rights reserved.

No part of this work may be reproduced or transmitted in any form or by any means, electronic, visual, or mechanical, including photocopying and recording, or by any information storage or retrieval system, without the prior written permission of the author. Requests for permission and inquiries should be addressed in writing to:

Maher Aref Abbas, M.D.
SYTAC HEALTH PUBLISHING
P.O.Box: 3027
Stanford, California 94309 USA

Library of Congress Catalog Card Number: 96-92946
ISBN 0-9656065-0-3

Printed in the United States of America.
First Edition: April 1997.
Cover Design: Sheryl Karas.

By the same author:

NOVELS
   * Children of Ambiguity

HEALTH BOOKS
   * College Students On The Go: Introduction to Healthy Living
   * The Mediterranean Diet: Olive Oil Cookery
   * Vegetarian Cuisine of Lebanon

Above books available at most bookstores or by contacting Sytac Health Publishing at above address.

I dedicate this book to my kind, loving, cheerful, inspiring and wise fathers Aref Abbas & Ralph Spiegl:
both of you were right --to see it with the heart, is the only way it makes sense.

And to Professor and Surgeon Willie Harshberg, M.D. --my gratitude for all the suffering you put me through, without which this book would not have been possible.

I am indebted to many people: to those who touched my life during internship year, to Dr. and Mrs. John Heymach, Mrs. Teresa Tracy, and Ms. Beth Tyner for editing this book, to Ms. Karen Evans for her emotional support, to Mrs. Linda Mccleve for her words of encouragement, to Mrs. Linda Buscaglia-Mohacsi for all the laughter we shared, to Miss Melissa Mazzei for all the good country music we enjoyed, to Don and Ginger from operating room number seven, and finally, to my former colleagues Drs. Michael Lutz and Douglas Gray, for all the wonderful, painful memories...

"Tomorrow, and tomorrow, and tomorrow, creeps in this petty pace from day to day, to the last syllable of recorded time; and all our yesterdays have lighted fools. The way to dusty death. Out, out, brief candle! Life's but a walking shadow, a poor player that struts and frets his hour upon the stage. And then is heard no more: it is a tale told by an idiot, full of sound and fury, signifying nothing."

William Shakespeare, MacBeth

FOREWORD

My decision, as a medical student, to enter radiology was primarily motivated by the fact that this was a rapidly growing field driven by an evolving technology that was playing an increasingly important role in medicine. I was also attracted to the great 9 to 5 lifestyle that every radiologist enjoyed. Not to mention the money --Radiology is the highest paid field in medicine, with radiologists earning up to a quarter million dollars a year or higher in salary. "Not bad," my father said to me, "for a photographer whose only job is to look at pictures!"

But before I could reap the benefits offered by the profession, I had to pay my dues: one year of clinical internship, followed by four years of radiology residency training. A year of internship didn't sound that bad, at least I didn't think so in the beginning. But little did I know at the time that that year was going to change my life forever!

Fresh out of medical school, I landed on the ward of one of the most prestigious American medical institutions. I was given a survival kit that included a pager, a meal card and a white coat. In the coat's pocket I found a list of sick and dying patients. When I was called to my first emergency, I told the nurse to page the patient's doctor --little did I realize that I was his doctor!

That's how I started my internship year: naive and idealistic. As it turned out, internship was nothing like I had imagined. It wasn't about medicine and science or anything else I had learned in medical school. It was about people and drama: the patients, the doctors, the nurses, the technicians, and death, misery, suffering, happiness, joy, music and SEX, lots of it!

I hope that you will enjoy this journey through the land beyond the magic scalpel, the land of doctors and their favorite associates, the attorneys! So, remember, although the events in this book are true, the honorable characters who you are going to meet, and the beloved institutions where they work, are fictitious. Any resemblance to actual persons, living or dead (especially dead!), or places is purely coincidental.

Maher Aref Abbas, M.D.
Palo Alto, California, April 1997

- One -

A black and white tag with my name on it: **Mick Baldi, M.D., Intern, Surgery.** I couldn't believe it. But it was true: I was a full-fledged physician at last.

I pinned the tag on my white coat and approached the nurse supervisor, who was sitting at the operating room information desk.

"Good morning. Can you please tell me where I can find Dr. Willie Harshberg?"

"He's in OR seven. Down the hallway to the right."

"Thank you," I waived, and continued walking.

"Hey, you? Where do you think you're going?" she shouted in a masculine voice.

"OR seven. Didn't you say that it was down this hallway to the right?"

"I did. But I didn't say that you could go there."

"I beg your pardon?"

"Don't you understand English?" she said, raising her voice as she got her fat ass off a crickety, wooden chair.

"Listen here, I'm Dr. Baldi from surgery..." I replied, pointing to my name tag.

"No, you look here, Baldi," she interrupted me. "I don't care who you are or where you come from. You're not going anywhere..."

"And may I ask you why?" I replied, desperately trying to be polite, while at the same time trying to gain some respect.

"Because I said so," she grunted.

"I see," I muttered, not knowing what else to say.

"And since I have your full attention right now, let me tell you about my rules around here," she said, as she walked around the desk, slowly dragging her three hundred pounds of hostility toward me. Her fat body generated more heat than a nuclear power plant. I was drenching in sweat.

"Institutional rules?"

"Engraved in stone and I won't repeat them twice," she barked. "I don't care what you think, doctor, but you'll follow my rules or else you'll have a year in hell! Never let me catch you in street clothes beyond this line," she said, pointing to a yellow line drawn across the hallway. "And if you think that

I'm mean, you wait 'til you meet my scrub nurses. Don't you ever dare piss them off."

"Is that all?" I asked.

"One more thing. If you have a complaint, don't tell me about it. Just fill out one of the forms over there and drop it in the employee's box," she said, showing me a plastic box hanging on one of the walls.

"Thank you for your welcoming introduction, nurse," I said, sarcastically. "Can I go see Dr. Harshberg now?"

"Karen. My name is Karen in case you haven't noticed yet," she replied, pointing to the sign on the desk with her name and title etched on it.

"As a matter of fact, I hadn't noticed. Your trim body was standing in the way!"

That comment didn't score me any brownie points. But I didn't care. I just wanted to get to the operating room. "The locker room is over there," she said, pointing to her left. "Make sure you have your entire surgical gear on before I see you walking down my hallway again. You may go now."

"Thanks," I mumbled.

"Mister Baldi?" she added.

"Yes, nurse Karen?"

"Have fun with the professor," she giggled, a triumphant smile spreading across her fat, nasty face. "I'm sure he's going to take care of you."

Karen's 'welcoming' remarks caught me off guard. I had heard that interns were at the bottom of the totem pole in the hospital hierarchy but this was ridiculous. I stopped by the restroom and spent about five minutes mustering up the courage to walk down the hallway again.

OR seven wasn't far. I entered without knocking. Good thing because there was a pretty intense conversation underway and I didn't want to get caught in the crossfire.

"Goddamn it, Cutter. Why in the fuck do you keep holding your needle like this? You're ripping this man's aorta apart. How many times do I have to tell you that you're doing it wrong? You hold your needle holder as if you were holding some kind of a dildo and vibrating it all over. Here, give me this," exclaimed Dr. Harshberg. He was donning rattlesnake boots and a cowboy hat, that was covered by a blue surgical cap. His oddball attire didn't surprise me because surgeons have a reputation for flaunting their personal eccentricities in the operating room. And Harshberg, being the chief of surgery, was no exception.

As soon as the tension eased, I decided to introduce myself. "Good morning. I'm Dr. Mick Baldi. I'm the new intern on your service."

Harshberg turned around slowly and scanned me from head to toe without saying a single word. Then he turned back and faced Cutter.

"Now, Cutter. You better get it straight this time. Look, here. This is the angle at which you need to sew the vessel. You go twice into the graft and once into the native artery. Do you think you can handle it? Do you think you're capable?"

"Yes, sir," replied Cutter, as he took hold of the instrument.

I wanted to see what they were doing, so I walked around the scrub nurse, who was standing next to the cowboy doctor and took a peek.

"Is that the pancreas next to the retractor?" I asked, pointing to the belly. No one seemed to care. No one answered. "It must be," I said to myself in a loud voice.

Harshberg looked at Cutter. "Tell this moron what's next to the fuckin' retractor. Also tell him that that was his last question for the day because I'm getting sick and tired of hearing his annoying voice."

"That's the duodenum," Cutter said, as he continued to work inside the patient's belly.

Embarrassed, I moved away form the surgeons and stood next to the anesthesiologist, who was minding his own business.

Deep down I was hurt. So far, my first day of internship wasn't going too well. I felt unwanted. But what annoyed me most was the boredom of the place. Twenty minutes of painful silence went by. Then I said another stupid thing. "Just in case you didn't catch my name, I'm Mick Baldi."

"DICK, WHO?" yelled Harshberg without looking up.

Nervous, I stuttered, "Miiick Baldi."

"Listen here, Dick Baldi," Harshberg said, wielding a big stainless steel clamp in the air. "Can't you fuckin' see that we're trying to save a man's life in here? Speak only when you're asked to do so. Besides, I don't fuckin' need to know your name. As far as I'm concerned, you're Rastus Internus, my intern. Is that understood?"

"Yes, sir," I replied, in a militaristic tone. I could feel my face turn instantaneously red in a split second.

"And when I tell you to shut up, you shut the fuck up and that's an order, son," he continued. "On my service we follow goddamn orders or patients die. It's that simple. And you better get used to it because your ass will be incarcerated on my service for the next year of your short life, whether you like it or not. This ain't medical school. This is about life and death. So the next time I tell you to shut the fuck up or do something, remember it's not a request, it's an order. I'll tell you when to work, I'll tell you when to eat and shit, and my patients and nurses will tell you when you get some sleep, understood?"

"Yes, sir."

"Meet Dr. Cutter Ungaman," he said pointing at the younger surgeon. "He's the chief resident of my service. His word is as good as mine, his orders should be followed to the letter. Understood?"

"Yes, sir."

"Now get the fuck out of my surgical field and sit in the corner over there. I don't want you contaminating this man's belly." He turned around to check on Cutter's progress. "WHAT IN THE HOLY FUCK DO YOU THINK YOU'RE DOING, FUCKHEAD?" he yelled, as he pushed Cutter's hands out of the man's belly and grabbed the bleeding aorta with his right hand. "Inger, get me the aortic clamp, quickly."

Inger, the scrub nurse, frantically handed it to him.

He yanked it out of her hand and tried to clamp the bleeding artery. "THIS IS THE WRONG CLAMP," he shouted. "You know that I never like to use DeBakey clamps."

"But Dr. Schinstein always does..."

"I DON'T GIVE A DAMN WHAT SCHINSTEIN DOES. AS A MATTER OF FACT, I COULD CARE LESS IF I SAW HIM WALKING AROUND THE HOSPITAL NAKED!" He threw the DeBakey clamp across the room, barely missing Cutter. "Give me my clamp."

"I'll get it for you," hurried Ron, the circulating nurse.

Harshberg looked at Cutter again. "What were you thinking?"

"No excuse, sir."

"Are you licensed to kill or cure, son?"

"Licensed to cure, sir," replied Cutter, standing at full attention.

"You need to concentrate on what you're doing. You know, Cutter, sometimes I wonder about you," Harshberg said, as he kept his right hand around the aorta. "You're in the last year of your training and you can't even put a blood vessel back together. What am I going to do with you? Dump you on the orthopedic surgery service?" Harshberg never thought highly of the orthopedists. He always called them dumb carpenters.

"No, sir. I would rather die than become an orthopod!"

"Here you go," Inger interjected, as she handed Harshberg the correct clamp.

He grabbed it with his left hand, rotated his body sideways against the table, and clamped the aorta. He spent the next half hour repairing the damage. Cutter didn't dare say a word.

"Looks good to me," said Inger, when Harshberg's job was done. She knew him the longest, and although he sometimes put her through hell, she was his favorite scrub nurse.

"It sure does, Inger. But his kidneys are going to be a problem. Our clamping time was too long. Cutter, go ahead and close his belly," he said, as he stepped away from the table, ripped off his apron, and took off his gloves. He always left the operating room in style. With a tip of the hat, he walked away like a cowboy riding into the sunset.

As soon as Harshberg left, Cutter asked the scrub nurse to play some country music.

"What a crazy morning!" he said. "It's one of those days. Are you all right?" he asked me.

"Yeah. Thanks."

"I'm sorry he gave you a hard time. Don't take it too personally. The man is a little anal sometimes."

"Is he always that mean?"

"Usually. But he's worse inside the operating room. It makes things kinda stressful for everyone else. You'll get used to him. Just follow his orders. Never argue or give your opinion. He's simply not interested."

"I see."

"Always say yes sir or no sir. Never give him details about anything. Make sure you're always on time. He wants you in the operating room before him. Make sure you hang the X-ray films to the light box. He gets really upset when they're not there."

"Do I have to scrub on all the cases?"

"Absolutely! You're also in charge of caring for all of the patients."

"Starting today?"

"Yeah. But don't worry. I'll back you up if you need me. My pager is always on. Did you meet Inger and Ron, yet? They're the best scrub nurses in the world and if you listen to what they tell you, you'll stay away from trouble."

"Welcome, Dr. Baldi. We're glad you're with us," the nurses both replied. I was surprised by how nice they were.

"And this is Dr. Gastein beyond the drapes."

The anesthesiologist stood up from his hidden spot at the head of the patient. "Nice to meet you."

"Thank you," I waved at him.

"Dr. Ungaman..."

"Please, call me Cutter," he interrupted.

"Cutter, what did Dr. Harshberg call me earlier?"

"When?"

"When he called me Dick Baldi."

"Oh," he laughed. "He called you Rastus. That's what he always calls his intern."

"What does it mean?"

"I don't know. Supposedly a southern word."

"Is that where he's from?"

"Texas. The man was born and raised a cowboy..."

- Two -

Harshberg was an asshole, no question about it. But he was a damn good surgeon. At the age of 35, he was the youngest doctor ever promoted to the position of chief of cardiovascular surgery at the American College of Legendary Surgeons, the ACLS, which was in effect, the highest honors in his field. Quite impressive for someone who grew up in Texas to be a cattleman!

In some ways, surgery was like baseball: many young players aspired to be in the major league but only a few made the cut. And fewer yet made it to the hall of fame. ACLS was the hall of fame for cardiovascular surgery. Many of the giants of modern surgery spent years training in its operating rooms.

Once he earned his place at the ACLS, Harshberg's goal became to train his future successor. Of all the young surgeons under him, he cared for one: Cutter Ungaman, his favorite student. He made him his protégé. That's why he came down hard on him everytime he made a mistake. He wanted him to become the best. Cutter wasn't the most talented in the group, but he had the right attitude: his zeal for cutting was immense. And that's the kind of attitude Harshberg liked, for he truly believed that every human being should die with a surgical scar on their chest or belly in order to get the most out of life!

Cutter worshipped two things: Harshberg, his mentor, and the operating room, his Mecca. Cutter felt depressed if a day would go by without being in OR seven for at least an hour or two. Once, he said that operating was like shaving to him --he needed to do it everyday in order to look and feel good!

"Mick, where are you?" Cutter asked, over the telephone.
"In the intensive care unit." It was the third week of my tour duty on Harshberg's service.
"Having fun yet?"
"Naah, just dicking around with Mr. Pisser's chest tube."
"Come on down, brother. You will have more fun over here. OR seven. It's a go."
"Mr. Jacob?"
"Yup. We're going to cut him tonight."

"But it's a belly case. Why don't we turf it to the general surgery boys?"

"Harshberg cracked his chest and fixed his heart ten years ago. Jacob is his patient. What can I say? Harshberg is a hero. He can do the heart and he can cut the belly, too!"

"So, it's going to be one of those chaotic nights?"

"Indeed, my friend. But have you ever asked yourself how boring life would be without chaos? We surgeons thrive on chaos."

"Shit."

"You damn radiologist," he grumbled, referring to my future training. "What would you rather be doing on a Friday night: watching TV at home or digging in someone's belly?"

"Digging in someone's belly, of course," I snickered.

"There you go, Rastus. You're starting to get the idea. Hurry now. My knife is ready to cut."

I looked up at the black and white clock inside OR seven. It was 11:30 p.m. Mr. Jacob was the second case of the evening. Cutter grabbed a pair of scissors and cut a large square in the blue drapes to uncover the patient's sick belly. Mr. Jacob was running out of luck. At the age of 57, his body was rotting away from a terrible cancer that was spreading fast. His stomach was filled with tumors and about five buckets worth of infected pus. His gut was twisted, ballooned, and inflamed. When I looked at the X-rays, I knew that he was a dying duck. All he needed was a compassionate drip of vitamin M: morphine.

Mr. Jacob should have died at home that night. But vomiting feces wasn't exactly a pleasant scene for his family, who rushed him to the hospital, where Cutter greeted them. He made their decision easy: do nothing and watch him defecate through his mouth and nose or cut his belly and fix the problem. The vitamin M discussion was never brought up for a very simple reason: at the ACLS, we loved to operate...

"KNIFE," shouted Cutter. His body was perched over Mr. Jacob like a vulture preying on a dead cadaver. He extended his left arm to his side. It was the beginning of the operating ritual. Inger firmly snapped the shiny stainless steel scalpel against the palm of his hand and Cutter seized the scalpel instinctively, never taking his eyes off Mr. Jacob's belly button.

"CUTTING AT 11:35," yelled Harshberg, who arrived at the table just a few moments earlier.

"Thank you, gentlemen," responded Dr. Gastein, the anesthesiologist. He verified the time, wrote it down in his log, leaned back in his chair, and went back to reading his Reader's Digest.

Cutter made an incision, which immediately drew criticism from Harshberg. "That incision is too whimpy. What type of an operation do you think we're doing in here?"

"Exploratory laparotomy, sir," Cutter answered.

"This is an exploratory procedure of the belly. We don't know how far or how deep we're going to have to cut this man," Harshberg said. "His belly needs to be wide open. Go ahead and increase your exposure. God Cutter, how many times do I have to remind you that you can compromise on love but you can't compromise on surgical exposure?"

That said, Cutter ran his knife up and down the patient's belly, cutting him wide open from his breast bone down to his pubis. "Cautery, Inger," he said, referring to the blue, pen-like device that is used to roast bleeding vessels. "Nothing gives me more pleasure than to zap those little suckers," Cutter exclaimed, as he looked at Harshberg, who smiled in return. He was glad to see that Cutter was enjoying himself.

A few minutes into the operation, Mr. Jacob's belly was sliced open and his muscles were pulled and strapped to each side of the table. A stream of yellowish liquid gushed out and splashed our sterile aprons.

"SUCK, RASTUS," Harshberg yelled. "Suck that fluid or we're going to drown in this pig's urine!" he continued, as he frantically grabbed my hand and pushed the sucking tube deep into Jacob's belly. Countless yards of small intestines kept creeping out. He tried to push them back into the belly. "I HATE THE SHITLANDS!" he exploded in disgust. Harshberg was referring to the intestines.

The cancer was everywhere. Cutter paused for a few seconds, then said, "This man is fucked big time."

"Yes, he is," echoed Harshberg, "but not the way he would have liked to have been fucked tonight. He's going nowhere except to intensive care. Our friend, Rastus, will show him what a good time he can have over there. Won't you, Rastus?"

"Yes, sir. I'll do whatever needs to be done," I replied.

Talented surgeons, but cruel bastards, I thought to myself. They even dared to make fun of this poor man's misery. Why couldn't they let him go in peace? Why slice him and dice him when they knew that fate would soon take its course?

"So, Cutter... What's your plan?" Harshberg asked, as he kept pushing the intestines back into the belly.

I prayed that Cutter would call the rest of the operation off. Or maybe that someone in the room would stand up for the rights of the dying man and stop the torture. But who was it going to be? Cutter was too eager to cut. I was too chicken to speak up. Dr. Gastein was too busy reading his Reader's Digest. The nurses were too involved in their mid-summer, Christmas-shopping conversation.

"Well..." Cutter hesitated.

"Rastus, goddamn it! Don't fag on me, son," complained Harshberg as I eased the retraction trying to rest my exhausted wrist. His hand was caught between the edge of the liver and the heavy retractor. "Concentrate on what you're doing and don't let go of that belly retraction."

"Yes, sir," I said, as I tightened my grip around the retractor. I looked inside Mr. Jacob's belly. The scene was unbearable. It was a mess beyond description. I thought about the Hippocratic oath I took upon graduating from medical school. I had pledged to do what was right for my patients under any circumstances. I was Jacob's physician as much as they were and my opinion should equal theirs, so I decided to speak up. "Sir, I'm a physician. I took my medical oath and pledged to..."

"Stop babbling, Rastus, and answer Ron," Harshberg said, as he kicked my leg with his cowboy boot.

Wrapped up in my own thoughts, I hadn't heard the telephone ring.

"Betsy from intensive care is calling. Mr. Evans hasn't been able to move his left side. What do you want her to do?" Ron was asking me.

Before I could choose whether or not to see the operation to its completion, Harshberg made the decision for me. "You're not being too helpful here. You're dreaming too much, son. Scrub out."

- Three -

Betsy was anxiously waiting outside of Mr. Evan's room. "Dr. Baldi, he hasn't been able to talk since nine o'clock this morning. The RN who took care of him during the day thought that the pain medication had clouded his mind. But he's been off of it now for seven hours. And I just noticed that he hasn't been moving his head to the left side at all. He's getting worse as we speak."

"No need to get excited yet," I replied. "He's still breathing, right?"

A dairy farmer from Minnesota, Mr. Evans was now lying in the intensive care at the ACLS, thousands of miles away from home. His head was tilted towards his right side, his eyes were shut, his mouth was partially open, and saliva was drooling on his neck. But he was breathing comfortably and his blood pressure was normal. I approached the left side of the bed and gently placed my hand on his forehead. "Mr. Evans, are you there? Can you hear me?" I asked, as I bent my body forward and spoke into his left ear. "Please open your eyes and look at me."

He opened his right eye and stared at the ceiling.

"Sir, talk to me. Do you know where you are?" No reply. Frustrated by the lack of response, I took him by the shoulders and shook him a couple of times.

"Moooooooo. Maaaaaaaaaa," he finally uttered.

"Sir, please tell me where you are," I asked again.

"Moooooooo. Maaaaaaaaaa," he repeated.

I inserted my right index and middle fingers in the palm of his left hand. "Mr. Evans? Squeeze my fingers with your left hand." No response. "SIR, SQUEEZE," I yelled directly into his ear.

"Moooooooo. Maaaaaaaaaa," he mumbled, as he moved his right hand. His left side appeared to be totally paralyzed.

"Fuck," I cursed, as I left the room.

Betsy rushed behind me. "What do you think?"

"He's a fuckin' cow. Didn't you hear him mooing?"

"Did he stroke?" she asked, ignoring my comment.

"What do you think? His brain is fried. He needs to have it imaged," I said, as I walked toward the unit secretary. "Hello there," I said. As usual, she was talking to her boyfriend on the telephone.

"Hold on, sweetie," she said, as she covered the telephone receiver. "Yes?"

"Call transport. Evans is going down to radiology to get his head scanned."

"I can't."

"What?" The last thing I needed was a unit secretary giving me a hard time.

"The scanners are all down. It's maintenance night."

I was furious. "This is the fuckin' ACLS! How can all the scanners be down at the same time?"

"Don't look at me like this, doctor. I only work here."

"Call an ambulance. We'll ship his ass off to the other hospital." I turned around and faced Betsy. "Call his wife. Tell her she needs to come here. I need to talk to her."

"I'll do it now."

"Thank you. I'm going back to the operating room. The boss isn't going to like this."

Harshberg hadn't seen Evans since his operation. As a matter of fact, he rarely saw any of his patients after he cut them. Sure, he always took credit for the successes. But I always took the blame for any complications.

"What do you think, Rastus?" Harshberg asked.

"Sir, he stroked. It must have happened over the last three hours or so. Cutter and I checked on him during our evening rounds and he was doing well."

"Poor bastard!" Harshberg said. "He thought that an operation was as simple as milking cows. Rastus," he continued, "do you remember seeing him in clinic with me?"

"Quite well, sir."

"What did I tell him?"

"He didn't need to have the surgery right away. He had pain in his leg but you assured him that he was in no immediate danger. You explained to him that his risks for a complication were quite high, especially with his heart and lung problems."

"I always thought that you were half-brain dead. But I'm amazed that you remembered. Now, Mr. Evans insisted on having the operation, didn't he?"

"Yes, sir, he did. He was scared of losing his leg."

"Shit happens. Post operative complications aren't totally unexpected. They're part of the job. I've learned to live with them. It's a price every surgeon pays. More operations mean more complications. I told you when you first came to my service that I have sick patients. Now you see. What do you want to do now?"

"Sir, I think we should get a CAT scan of his head. The machine is down at our facility so I want to send him to the other hospital to get it. I'd like to consult with the neurologist on duty, with your permission, of course."

"Rastus, you don't need my permission. You're in charge of your patients and responsible for them. Go do what you have to do."

"Thank you. Sir, if it's a blood clot in his head that caused his stroke and not a bleed, can I dissolve it? It might improve some of his paralysis," I suggested.

"How the hell would I know? Discuss it with the neurologist. He knows more about the brain than I'll ever know or care to know. Do what you have to do and come back here. Quite frankly, we're getting lost in Jacob's shitlands and we need you."

I headed for the door.

"RASTUS?" he yelled.

"SIR?" I turned around, and stood at attention.

"I like the way you call me 'sir'," he said, laughing. "Cutter and I were discussing that you would make a good surgeon. You're a SIR MAN!"

"YES, SIR," I replied.

"Why don't you give up your radiology dream and stay with us next year?"

"Five more years with you, sir?" I smiled. "Not a chance!"

"Goddamn radiologists," I heard him say, on my way out.

- Four -

In medical school, the chief of the intensive care unit once told me that neurologists are worthless professionals because they spend countless hours examining patients and intellectually masturbating over their conditions without making the slightest difference in their care. He went on to tell me that a CAT scanner was worth a room full of neurologists.

I was reminded of that conversation when I paged the neurologist on duty. Fifteen minutes and three unanswered pages later, I decided to call him at home.

"Hello?" he answered.
"Dr. Thalamus?"
"Who's this?"
"Dr. Baldi. I'm the intern on the Harshberg service."
"What do you want?"
"Dr. Harshberg asked me to consult with you on a patient."
"At this fuckin' hour? What time is it?"
"Almost one o'clock, sir."
"What's so urgent that it can't wait 'til morning?"
"Mr. Evans. We operated on him two days ago. We cut down on his pain medication because he was gorked out. Now his left side has shut down. The question is..."
"Yes, he stroked. Why are you calling me?"
"Because his brain is in question. Dr. Harshberg is a cardiovascular surgeon and not a brain specialist. He wants you involved..."
"He stroked. There ain't much I can offer him at this hour. I'll see him in the morning. Anything else?"
"Sir, the question is thrombolytics. If it's a blood clot and not a bleed that caused his stroke, should we thin his blood and dissolve it? We can ask the neurointerventional radiologist to open up the clogged vessel with a balloon catheter."
"Where did you hear this bullshit?"
"At Stanford, sir. They're doing it with good success."
"That's Stanford. The boys out on the West Coast are a bunch of crazy, aggressive and experimental fucks. I'm not comfortable with that sort of stuff. You thin his blood and next thing you know he's bleeding into his head or his leg where you cut him. What did Harshberg say about his leg?"

"He said that between saving his brain or bleeding into his leg, screw the leg! We can always go back again and fix his leg but his brain only has one chance."

"I see. So what would you like to do?"

"You need to see him, sir. You're the brain specialist."

"Do whatever you want. You can't be faulted either way. He already lost half of his brain. The worst thing that can happen to him is he will die. I'll see him in the morning and leave a note in his chart," he said, as he hung up the telephone.

Irresponsible asshole, I thought to myself. I wasn't a neurologist.

I stood in the intensive care unit thinking about what to do next. I cared about Evans. If there was any chance of recovering some of his brain function, I was willing to do it. But what if I killed him in the process of helping?

"Dr. Baldi, Mrs. Evans is in the waiting area..." Betsy said from behind. "Would you like to talk to her now?"

I didn't want to talk to her just now, but I had no choice. As I made my way over to the waiting room, I wondered what I'd tell her. Should I tell her Harshberg thought that her husband was an unfortunate bastard? Or should I tell her that Thalamus valued his sleep more than her husband's brain?

"It's good to see you," I said. "Sorry you had to come here this late. Your husband's condition took a turn for the worse. He suffered a stroke."

"Is it serious?" she asked, suddenly pale-faced.

"We're quite concerned about him. We'll do our best to help him out. It's really quite unfortunate," I said, with a sympathetic smile. "Do you remember our discussion in the clinic?"

"His leg was hurting him so much. He thought that the surgery would help him. Has Dr. Harshberg seen him tonight?"

"He did," I lied. "He examined him, then asked me to follow him closely."

"Do you think he needs to be seen by a brain doctor?"

"I've already called our best neurologist at the ACLS, Dr. Thalamus. He's on his way right now," I said, lying for the second time.

"Oh, Lord," she sobbed.

"Don't worry, Mrs. Evans. I'll take good care of your husband. If you'll excuse me now, I have to go back to the operating room. I'll see you later."

I stood outside OR seven, my mouth covered with a clean surgical mask. Through the window I saw Harshberg and Cutter at work. They were busy slicing and dicing Mr. Jacob. I felt awful as I scrubbed in. Just thinking about Mr. Evans made me cry. I had lied. I had let down my father who had always taught me to be honest. But what else could I have done? I did the best I could to get through the situation. Being responsible for sick patients wasn't an easy thing to do.

As I entered the operating room, I pledged to myself that I was going to pull Mr. Evans through. Mr. Jacob presented an entirely different situation. With my arms raised in the air and water dripping from my elbows, I walked toward Inger, who handed me a blue towel so that I could dry my arms. I slipped into a sterile gown and approached the cancer-ridden patient. I was his only hope and I was determined to put an end to his suffering.

- Five -

"Is everything squared away with Evans?" Harshberg asked, as I made my way toward the operating table.

"Yes, sir. He's getting his head scanned. Thalamus is involved. I've spoken with the wife and given the nurse a couple of Valiums to relax!"

He didn't really care about the details, so that's all I told him.

"Good work, Rastus. While you were gone trying to decide what to do with Evans' brain, we've been trying to decide what to do with Jacob's shitlands. It's quite a challenge. We don't know what's intestine and what's tumor. Look here," he pointed to the right side of his belly, "even his abdominal wall is seeded with cancer. We just put a hole in his bowel. Rastus, this man had more shit pouring into his belly than I'd ever seen. Cutter did a good job sewing it back together."

"More irrigation?" Cutter asked.

"His belly is polluted with shit. IRRIGATE IT, SON. IRRIGATE IT," Harshberg yelled. "Do I have to remind you again about the solution to pollution?"

"*The solution to pollution is dilution...*" sang Cutter.

"Frankly, we can't do much more for him," Harshberg said. "We relieved one of his many obstructions. I think I'm going to call it quits. I'll talk to his family. Rastus, you go ahead and close the belly with Cutter. This was a long and tough day, boys. Thank you."

"Dr. Harshberg, are you going to examine Mr. Evans on your way out? I believe he should be back any minute now."

"No, Rastus. I don't need to see him. I fixed his leg. I can't fix his brain."

"I understand, sir," I replied. Turning to Jacob, I asked Harshberg, "sir, how aggressive do you want me to be in supporting him?"

"I don't know. What does Cutter want to do?"

"He's going to be tough to manage in intensive care. His pressure is definitely going to be a problem because of bleeding. It's hard to know how much blood he's going to need..." Cutter said.

"There's a lot I can do for him. What's appropriate?" I asked again, hoping Harshberg would let me be merciful.

"Frankly, I don't care," Harshberg admitted. "See you in the morning," he turned around and looked at Dr. Gastein. "Shit! He's sleeping again. RISE AND SHINE ANESTHESIA! IT'S DOUGHNUT TIME," he yelled, and laughed as he left the room.

Poor Gastein jumped off his chair and dropped his Reader's Digest on the floor. "Asshole." I heard him mumble.

"Vicryl suture to Dr. Baldi. Let's close this depressing mess. Ron, let's hear some country goodies," Cutter ordered.

"Right away, Dr. Ungaman. What would we do without country music!" the southerner replied. Ron knew every country music song. And with his long hair and large mustache --protruding from both sides of his face mask-- he looked like your typical country singer.

"How aggressive do you want me to be with Jacob's care?" I asked Cutter.

"*Sitting with my dog on the porch, both of us have been waiting for you honey, with his sweet eyes you've always loved, he looks at me and asks me how soon you'll be coming back...*" Cutter sang with the music. He ignored my question.

"Cutter, come on," I said, raising my voice. I stopped sewing the belly and looked at him.

He quit singing. "What do you want from me?"

"What do I want from you? Look at him. He's fuckin' butchered. Let's stop it here. This man's suffering shouldn't be prolonged. Harshberg doesn't care what happens to him. Let's pull the plug right now, right here. We'll tell him that he crashed on us."

The anesthesiologist and the two nurses waited for Cutter's response. "If you're looking for answers, don't look at me. I'm here to learn how to operate. I did my work. You're in charge of his care now. Do what you think is right," he finally answered, ignoring my request to let go of Mr. Jacob. "I'm taking off. Finish up here and I'll meet you in intensive care at five," he replied, as he took off his sterile apron and walked out of the room, thoroughly exhausted.

Gastein stuffed his Reader's Digest in his pocket. We got Mr. Jacob off the operating table and transferred him to his intensive care unit bed. He ended up five rooms away from Mr. Evans. Gastein gave a full report to Silvia, the ICU nurse, one of the best around.

I sat at the desk in front of Jacob's room and looked at him. He was hooked to a breathing machine and his green stomach juices were flowing through a tube shoved in his left nostril. His body was tangled up by a bundle of lines supplying him with blood products, antibiotics, fluids, and medications. Two drains were sticking up from his belly, emptying a mixture of shit and tumors.

Silvia was struggling with all the lines and tubes. She tried to identify and mark each one of them. She seemed stressed. I was too. Mr. Jacob was a big mess. He was suffering.

I walked up to Silvia. "I suppose the anesthesiologist told you all about the case."

"He did. Looks like Harshberg and Cutter dumped the patient on you. I have no respect for Harshberg. I've seen him chew out his residents in the intensive care unit before." Silvia wasn't one to hide her dislike.

"It's hard for doctors to decide what to do sometimes," I said, trying to defend his action. "This man is sick. He needed help. He came to the surgeons. What do you expect them to do? If Jacob's family would have sought the help of a medical doctor, it would have been different. Maybe he just needed the help of a rabbi, one who could have held his hand tonight, as he passed away peacefully. But instead, his family brought him to the surgeons. Harshberg has good intentions. He tried to do what he thought was best for this man."

Silvia was surprised by my answer. She knew well how Harshberg put me down every chance he got. And now, I was standing up for him. In reality, I wasn't. As a doctor, I was entitled to question the actions of other doctors. But that was something to be done in private, a principle I had already failed to observe by questioning Cutter in front of Inger and Ron. "Dr. Baldi, I respect you. I know what position you're in. What are you going to do?" she said.

I hesitated.

"Are you going to do the right thing?" she pressed on.

"What's the right thing, Silvia? Harshberg told me to do the right thing, Cutter told me to do the right thing, and now you are wondering whether I will do the right thing, damn it."

"Didn't they teach you anything at Stanford?"

"Honesty and compassion towards my patients. But this is the real world, Silvia. It's not medical school where I can turn to some professor or some text for answers. I have to find the answer and live with it. Help me."

"If Mr. Jacob were your father, what would you do?"

"I would find him a rabbi and bring my family here tonight. I wouldn't do anything aggressive at this point. Just a sweet drip of morphine and let him go join his father and grandfather," I replied, softly.

"Dr. Baldi, his pressure is dropping. Do you want me to start a drip to bring it back up?" she asked.

Silvia was pushing me. I looked at Mr. Jacob and then at the monitor. His systolic pressure was now eighty.

"So, do you want to treat his low pressure?"

I looked at her. Her face was sweet and gentle. I looked down and took my glasses off to rub my aching and sleepy eyes. "No, Silvia. You know what to do."

"Is this a verbal order?" she asked.

"Yes, it is," I said, firmly.

"Can I give you a verbal order, Dr. Baldi?"

"I beg your pardon?"

"I don't see a rabbi around here. Please hold his hand and pray. I'll go get the morphine drip."

Nurses never gave doctors orders. Yet I listened to Silvia because she had the courage to do what three doctors didn't dare do --let this man die in peace. I held his right hand and told him that it was okay for him to go. Silvia returned with the morphine.

"Thank you, Silvia."

I walked away, happy with the decision I had made, but worried about the consequences of my action. My job was at stake.

"Dr. Baldi..." Silvia called out from the room. "You're a good man."

I looked back. The drip was already hung and he was on his way to a peaceful death.

- Six -

Surgeons and fighting marines have several things in common. They follow orders without questioning them and perform their duties with focused determination and infectious enthusiasm. Their incredible stamina also allows them to operate under the worst conditions, such as hunger and lack of sleep.

At five in the morning, Cutter arrived in the intensive unit, clean-shaven and dressed in a recently ironed suit. He looked refreshed and ready for another day of cutting.

"Good morning, Mick," he said, as he handed me a cup of hot, black coffee. "You sure look like shit!"

"Believe me I feel worse than I look. But I can't complain much. I survived the night and so did my patients, so that's all that matters," I said.

"It's part of the ritual, brother. You have to pay your dues just like everyone else. But trust me, it will pay off in the end," he replied, with his hands inside his pant pockets. "How are the unit players?"

"Sick as usual. The ruptured aneurysm kept me busy for a while. His blood pressure was all over the place."

"I figured that was going to happen. It's a miracle that he's still alive five days after we cut him. Let me tell you, these Irish drunkards are tough!"

"Tell me about it. At the rate things are going I'll probably be dead before him!"

"You're doin' well, brother. Just follow orders and don't ask too many questions and you'll survive the year," he added.

"So what happened with farmer Evans?"

"He stroked his temporal lobe. Probably a clot in his middle cerebral artery."

"No bleeding? Good for him." He looked down at his medical chart. "So, did you blast his brain with blood thinners?"

"What do you think, Cutter?" I teased.

"Oh, come on, it's too early for guessing games. Did you do it?"

"You know the answer," I replied.

His face lit up with excitement. "You aggressive son of bitch! You're a fuckin' cowboy! You're sure you don't wanna be a surgeon?"

"Definitely not," I answered.

"You don't think that surgery is good enough for you, Mister X-ray?!"

"Look, I didn't dissolve his clot."

"Why not?" he asked, sounding a bit disappointed.

"Put yourself in my shoes. If a neurologist and a cardiovascular surgeon couldn't decide what to do for the patient, how could you expect a burnt out intern to do so? Cutter, thrombolytics aren't exactly a piece of candy. This stuff kills people."

"I hear you."

"Did I ever tell you the story about the Armenian man I met when I was a student?" I asked him. "At the age of eighty-two he was allowed to leave the communist block to join his two sons in California. His right hip was killing him. Terrible arthritis. Three days after getting out there, they give him a new hip. Right after the surgery he had a heart attack because of a blockage in one of his heart arteries. A bunch of smart specialists gathered around his bed to decide whether they should dissolve the clot or not. Big decision. And you know what?"

"They didn't do it..." he predicted.

"Wrong," I said. "They did. The orthopedic surgeon took the heat because it was his patient. He gave him the blood thinner and the man bled into his hip in the middle of the night. His blood pressure dropped and his heart arrested. I banged on his chest for awhile. He kissed his eighty-two years good-bye and landed in the morgue that same night."

Cutter seemed touched by the story.

"Mr. Evans is half paralyzed but at least he's still with us this morning," I continued. "Thalamus will see him and we'll take it from there. Maybe he'll get better."

We turned our attention to Mr. Jacob. Silvia was at the end of her night shift. The morphine drip was still running. It took Cutter a couple of minutes to realize what I had done. His sudden nervousness was quite noticeable.

"He seems stable," he finally said.

"Stable?" I questioned. "The man is dying, Cutter. He's taking his last breaths. The morphine did him a lot of good."

"I didn't mean stable," he mumbled, "I meant peaceful. How about his blood pressure?"
"What about it?"
"Too low."
"Cutter, are we going to treat a dead man?" I paused. "You did the best you could in the operating room. His cancer was beyond cure."
"Ugly fuckin' tumors! Cancer is nasty, brother. But you have to admit one thing though: it was funny watching how pissed off the boss was, trying to push the shitlands back into that belly. I was having a ball!" he said, grinning. After a pause, he added, "you did the right thing. Let's hope he dies before Harshberg comes in this morning."
I was relieved by his support. "Hey, Cutter. I appreciate you backing me on this one."
"This whole thing was a goddamn mess from the start," he replied. "But it's over. That's the one thing I love about surgery: it's always over whether they die or get better. Cut and run. That's the name of the game! Let's go check on the ward patients."

Half way there, Cutter's pager went off. "Shit. It's too early for an emergency," he cried out, as he looked at his watch.
We hurried to the next ward, where he picked up the nearest phone. The conversation was brief. I heard him say 'yes, sir' a few times. He hung up and walked towards me with an air of disappointment.
"What's wrong?" I asked.
"The boss... He wants the care of Mr. Jacob transferred to the critical care team. He called their consultant already."
"What?" I said in disbelief. "Critical care team? Jacob is dead. Why didn't you try to convince him?"
"I can't argue with him."
"Why not?"
"You talk like an idiot sometimes. Do you know who Harshberg is?"
"I don't give a fuck who he is!"
"He's one of the most powerful people this place has ever known. The ACLS runs because of people like him," Cutter replied curtly, "and it may be that you don't give a fuck about who he is, but let me tell you something here you little spoiled brat... He's the boss and you just follow his fuckin' orders..."

"How about Mr. Jacob? Aren't we held accountable to him and his family? You know this shit ain't right. We're his doctors too."

"We follow orders at the ACLS. One day you'll give your own orders to your subordinates..."

"Orders? I don't give a damn about orders. We're here to serve people, not just follow orders! Do you think it's fair that Harshberg butchered Mr. Jacob's belly and left him in this mess?"

"You just don't get it, do you?" Cutter quickly replied. "This place isn't about what's fair or not. It's about saving lives and advancing the science of medicine." Cutter was getting angry now. He disliked my lack of respect to my superiors. "If you want fairness and justice, just go across the street to the church."

"Harshberg's doing this because he doesn't want him to die on our service," I said, in a bitter tone. "You, surgeons, hate it when a patient dies on your service. You look bad when it happens."

Cutter was fed up. "Whatever. I'm not going to argue with you anymore. Frankly, I don't give a damn either way. If you have a problem, go ahead and call Harshberg."

"But you're the chief resident..."

"I am and I'm going to get ready for the operating room... I'll see you there."

I was speechless. I was Mr. Jacob's doctor, yet there was nothing I could do for him. Not even a peaceful death. I rushed downstairs to the intensive care unit wishing to see him dead before the critical care team laid a hand on him. But it was too late. They had just arrived. Their first order of business was Mr. Jacob and their senior resident was the first to show up in his room.

"I know that Dr. Harshberg asked you to take over Jacob's care. I've been providing him with comfort care over night. He's ready to go," I said. But my attempt to persuade him to take non-aggressive measures was futile.

"If he was truly ready to go, why did you operate on him last night?" the senior resident asked.

"It was a mistake. This man didn't need an operation in the first place. Please keep the morphine running," I begged.

He completely ignored my request. "Look at this blood pressure," he said in horror, while looking at the monitor. "Silvia, get a neosynephrine drip. His pressure is unacceptable. I'm going to call my intern. This man needs a heart catheter."

- Seven -

"Good morning. Any magic pills for baldness, yet?" I inquired as I took my baseball cap off.

From the time I first arrived at the ACLS three months earlier, I had been visiting Fred every two weeks. He was my barber. I kept coming back to his shop because he was always very delicate with my hair and quite sensitive to the fact I was growing bald by the week.

Fred was a native of Arizona. He had cut hair for about forty of his sixty years of life. He was a typical southwestern man with dark glasses, polyester pants, cowboy boots and hat, and a large leather belt with a nickel buckle, that was heavy enough to give anyone low back pain! His hair was gray with a tinge of yellow in the front, a reminder of the heavy cigarette smoking he had done most of his life. A Marlboro packet always sat inside the upper left pocket of his shirt. His shop was one of the oldest in town, with its decor reflective of the sixties. Most of his customers were senior citizens and some of the magazines piled up on his coffee table dated back to 1966, the year I was born.

"Dr. Baldi, it's always a pleasure to see you. Here, let me take your glasses," he said as I sat in the chair next to the window. "So how would you like it done today?"

I looked at my head in the mirror. Fred reached for his scissors.

"How would you like it?" he asked again.

"Fred, you always ask me the same question. By now you should know what to do with my balding head."

"I suppose you want the modified senior citizen cut again."

"Make me beautiful, Fred. When I walk in the hospital people sometimes confuse me for a patient on chemotherapy. I'm afraid that there won't be much hair left for you to cut in the near future," I joked.

Fred was a passionate and talented artist. His skilled hands always managed to make the best of my repulsive scalp. He was very creative at concealing my baldness by reflecting patches of long hair from either side of my head to cover the middle. Without Fred's help, my social life would have suffered. In addition to making me look good, he always listened to my concerns regarding baldness and made me feel better. In many ways, my frequent visits to his shop were similar to psychotherapy sessions. The only difference was that Fred only charged me ten dollars a visit!

"So Fred, any magic pills yet?" I asked again, for the umpteenth time.

"OH, YES!" he exclaimed. "Pills for magic hope! They're magic for those who make money selling them, but they only give hope to those who buy them. I have yet to see any hair grow on any of my customers who take them. All those years, all those lotions and potions, and all I've seen is baldness. Let's hope for a miracle, Dr. Baldi, but I don't think it's going to be during my lifetime."

"How about Proscar?" I asked.

"What is it?"

"A drug used in older men to treat big prostates. Proscar stops the body from making testosterone. Since baldness is caused by too much testosterone, someone thought that Proscar might stop hair from falling off..."

"How interesting!"

"Yeah. Someone in San Francisco is conducting a study with young men," I continued.

"How much do you need to take?"

"One pill every day."

"For how long?"

"Supposedly for life. Otherwise, the hair would fall off."

"For life? Hum!" He paused. "I don't know, Dr. Baldi, but I would be scared if I were a young man."

"Why?"

"It's a hormone thing. When you give it to cows they get cancer. Hell, we do too after we eat their meat..."

"But this is different. Cows and people are different..." I tried to explain.

"No, they're not. I grew up the son of a cattleman and I can assure you that cows and people are the same..."

"But Fred..." I replied, only to be interrupted again.

"I don't like the idea of a hormone," he said. "And quite frankly, anyone who's willing to take it for life must be crazy."

"But could you imagine the beautiful hair it would grow?"

"How about its effect on your prostate? Son, you don't know what it's like to have prostate problems."

"I think it's safe in young men."

"How about cancer? What would people say? He grew a head full of hair but died young of cancer. I mean, come on, Dr.

Baldi!" he exclaimed, as he raised his hands up in the air. He was willing to argue all day.

"I guess you have a point, Fred."

"Don't worry, doc. You got the money. Between your hair or your wallet, most ladies would prefer your wallet."

"No, I don't have any money."

"I meant, you will have it someday. That's guaranteed."

"It's easy for you to say that money means more to women. Your hair is thick like a sheep!"

"It's only hair. Just don't worry..." he tried to reassure me.

"Worry? Did you know that Julius Caesar spent the eves of many major battles worrying about his baldness instead of his enemy?"

"Well I can't do much for Mr. Caesar," he petted me on the right shoulder, "but I can do a lot for you. Just give me a few minutes and you'll walk out of this place looking like a million dollars. Look," he pointed to two blondes walking outside his shop, "the ladies are already lining up for you."

Fred always had a way of making people feel better. He was full of optimism, happiness, and humor.

"You're wonderful, Fred," I said, as I looked at him in the mirror.

"I'm just a barber," he replied, humbly. "By the way, can I ask you a question?"

"Sure."

"I was wondering about you doctors. I've never met a doctor who wasn't bald. Why is that?"

"We worry too much."

"I think you're right. Knowing too much can be to one's detriment. Let me tell you something," he said as he put down the scissors and grabbed the clippers, turned them on, and started shaving my neck, "everytime I see my doctor he complains about my smoking. He's worried that I'm going to get lung cancer. Hell, I'm not..."

"I would be worried, too," I said.

"You really believe that cigarettes are bad?"

"Of course."

"Can you name the country where people smoke the most?" he quizzed me. His stinky smoker's breath overwhelmed my nostrils.

"China?"

"No, it's Greece. What's more interesting however, is the fact that Greece has the lowest incidence of lung problems in the world. We're not talking about Europe here, we're talking about the whole world. Now if smoking was truly bad, those Greeks should have been dropping dead like fruit flies. But they're not," he said lifting both of his eyebrows. "What's your explanation, doc?"

Fred was always skeptical of the medical profession.
"I don't know what to tell you," I responded.
"Do you know what it boils down to, Dr. Baldi?"
"What, Fred?"
"Luck. Just luck," he replied with a smile. "Some people can do things and get away with them and some can't."

Fred handed me his small mirror. "What do you think? You look terrific, doc."

As usual, he had done a good job. As a reward to himself, he reached into his shirt pocket and pulled out the Marlboro packet.

I got up and pulled a ten dollar bill out of my wallet.
"Your business is always appreciated, Dr. Baldi," he said, as he reached for the money. I always tipped him an extra dollar. "Just remember, some people can get away with things," he said, winking his right eye.

"Are you trying to tell me something?"
"Well, son. Maybe you wanna consider that hormone Proscar. Maybe you'd get away with the side effects."

I smiled and took off with some hope.

- Eight -

Dr. Harshberg loved to give orders and establish rules. And one of his favorite rules was the twelve and two: twelve consecutive days and nights on hospital duty followed by a weekend off to rest. But two days off out of every fourteen wasn't enough. That's why I took advantage of every rare opportunity I had to catch up on my sleep.

One of those opportunities was the early morning surgical conference. I always sat in the back of the auditorium and leaned my sleepy head against the wall. It was a safe and peaceful place to snooze as the mighty surgeons recounted their heroic stories of the week. Most of the conferences were supplemented with a set of slides from the operating theater. With the room lights off, the bloody slides were projected on a large white screen. The result was an unusual and hypnotic visual effect, especially for the sleep-deprived interns!

That morning was no exception. I was in such a deep sleep, I didn't realize that the talk was over.

"WAKE UP, RASTUS!"

I opened my eyes. Cutter was staring me in the face.

"Son, if people saw the way you sleep during these conferences, they'd think you're suffering from a sleeping disorder," Harshberg chimed in.

I got up and adjusted my tie. Both of them were laughing. They looked cute in their matching black, white and gray checkered suits. It was obvious Cutter had bought a suit to match the boss' suit.

"The hospital on-call schedule is brutal on your service," I said, as we started walking down the hallway. "I seldom get any sleep."

"Brutal?" he asked, sarcastically. "Rastus, you don't even know what brutal means. For my entire general surgery training at Massachusetts General Hospital in Boston, I was on-call every other night. No weekends, no holidays. Every other night, son. But I'll admit that I did complain at the time."

"I would have complained, too," echoed Cutter, who kissed ass a lot.

"I complained because I was missing half of all the good cases on my nights off!" Harshberg interjected, with a straight-face. If he was anything like he is now, I'm sure he did complain when he had time off.

"Today is clinic day," Harshberg said, changing the subject. "We need to book a lot of people for surgery next week. The name of the game is to recruit fast. Get active, boys," he added with an enthusiastic tone. "Cutter, give me a quick rundown of our hospital service."

Although I managed the patients on the service, Harshberg always requested his update from Cutter. That's the way the hierarchy was set up in Boston, and that's the way he wanted it on his service. Cutter rarely had a clue as to what was going on with all the patients. But he was good at impressing Harshberg with his short positive assessment of the patients. That was the best kind of update for Harshberg, who didn't care to know much.

"Most people are doing well," Cutter reported. "Mr. Evans has shown some signs of improvement in the last three days. When I asked him yesterday where he was, he thought he was in a barn."

"What does the neurologist think?" Harshberg asked.

"Not much. He left a two-line note on the chart yesterday, that read, *Patient thinks he's in a barn. Will continue to monitor his neurological progress.* That was his assessment," Cutter replied.

Harshberg turned around and pointed at me with his right index finger. "Rastus, never consult with the neurologists in the future. They're useless. I mean look here. We consulted with Thalamus. He wasted a few thousand dollars in imaging studies between CAT scans and expensive MRIs, and charged the patient a few hundred dollars in consultation fees. And what does he tell us? That the patient thinks he is in a barn. That's bullshit."

"Big bullshit!" echoed Cutter.

"What ended up happening to Jacob?" Harshberg inquired, as we walked out of the intensive care unit.

"The critical care boys played with his medications and drips for two days. He continued to worsen. Last night his heart stopped. They tried to resuscitate him for a good hour and a half but he didn't respond. So they let him go."

Beautifully said, I thought to myself. Did they have a choice? They didn't let him go, he went and they had no way of bringing him back. The torture was over.

"I just can't understand why they were so aggressive with his care. He was dying. I asked them to give him supportive care," Dr. Harshberg said, trying to justify the torture he himself had sentenced Mr. Jacobs to during the last few days. "I suppose they misinterpreted what I said."

Coward, I called him in silence. He knew exactly what he had done to the patient. Yet he didn't have the courage to admit it.

"Anything else this morning?"

"Yes. There's a patient on the medicine service we were asked to see. Her name is Mrs. Duffy. She's a fifty-eight year old woman with a long-standing history of smoking. They spotted a mass in her lung on one of her chest X-rays. It's in her right upper lung. They're not sure if it's cancer or infection, like tuberculosis or fungus. The radiologist was reluctant to biopsy it with a needle because it's close to the major blood vessels. They're asking us to see her for an open chest procedure to remove the mass," Cutter said, raising his eyebrows.

"Where is she?"

"Third floor."

"Let's go see her," Harshberg said.

As I walked behind Dr. Harshberg, I noticed that his legs were disproportionately larger than the rest of his body. His neck was always tilted forward and the curvature of his chest was more exaggerated than I thought. I always wondered whether the weight of his exquisite cowboy hat was the culprit.

We stopped at Mrs. Duffy's room.

"Good morning. I'm Dr. Harshberg from surgery. These are my two assistants, Drs. Ungaman and Baldi. Your doctors have asked us to see you regarding that mass of yours. It's sitting in your lung. They're concerned it's cancer."

"But it might be something else," Mrs. Duffy added, in a hopeful tone.

"Yes, it might be, but your doctors are concerned. There's only one way we can tell what it is, and that is to take it out. When in doubt, we always take it out. Don't we, boys?"

"Absolutely. We never like to live in doubt!" Cutter reciprocated.

"Can you be sure that it's cancer?" she asked.

Dr. Harshberg smiled again. "We surgeons may not always be right, but we're always sure."

"I'm really scared of an operation."

"I would be too. But we need to know what's sitting in your chest..." he tried to explain.

"Can't we wait and see how things go?" she asked, nervously.

"No, ma'am."

"But you don't know what it is. If it's not cancer, then the surgery would be unnecessary, wouldn't it?"

"Yes, it would be."

"I'd hate to undergo an unnecessary procedure," she added.

Dr. Harshberg was loosing his patience. Most of his hospital consultations lasted three minutes or less and this one was going overtime.

"I agree with you. As far as I'm concerned, I hate to do unnecessary surgery, too. I like to see real pathology, serious diseases. I can't tell if yours is real or not, unless I cut your chest open and take out what's sitting in it."

Mrs. Duffy was frightened. She looked at Cutter and me. "I'd hate to have my chest opened for an unnecessary reason. Wouldn't you agree?"

Dr. Harshberg was fed up with her. "I agree with you one hundred percent. Did you schedule her already?" he asked Cutter.

"Next Friday. First case at seven-thirty in the morning."

"Good," he turned around and looked at Mrs. Duffy. "We have a date in the operating room next week. It won't take long, Mrs. Duffy. For your sake, I hope that you have cancer. I sure would hate to do an unnecessary operation and waste my time," he said, staring at her with his steely eyes.

She was taken aback by his comment and started crying as we exited the room.

A few moments later, Dr. Harshberg realized that something had gone wrong. "Boys, did I say to this lady what I thought I just said?"

Cutter hesitated for a moment, then said, "you hate to do unnecessary surgery, so you wished her cancer."

"Shit," he swore. "I suppose that wasn't a nice thing to say to an old lady. Go back, Cutter, and fix it. Say whatever you need to say. Make her feel better. Rastus and I will meet you in clinic."

"Yes, sir," he responded as he turned around and headed toward her room.

"You know, Rastus, she made me say it," Harshberg said, without remorse. "Why couldn't she understand that in this world, when in doubt, we always cut it out!"

- Nine -

Dr. Harshberg believed that the most important aspect of surgical training was learning how to recruit the patients. Why recruit? Simply because non-distressed, clinic patients never volunteered to be cut open! They had to be actively recruited to sign up for one or more of the many exotic procedures on the Harshberg menu.

"Good morning, Mr. Peterson. I'm Dr. Harshberg from surgery. Allow me to introduce Drs. Ungaman and Baldi."
As usual, I carried the recruiting folder with all the legal forms.
"Three of you to see me? I'm really flattered," Peterson replied, nervously. He looked at his wife, who was sitting next to him, then turned around to face us. "Am I paying each of you separately?"
"No, sir. You get three for the price of one. These are my boys. I need them to keep me out of trouble," Harshberg chuckled.
"Do you often get in trouble?" Peterson asked.
"Not as often as I'd like," Harshberg joked. The lighthearted conversation seemed to have calmed Peterson's nerves a bit.
Cutter seemed to enjoy the conversation so far.
"I see... Oh, this is my wife, Florence," Peterson said, as he gently laid his right hand on her shoulder.
"Nice to meet you, ma'am."
"The pleasure is mine," she replied.
Harshberg's tone became serious as he turned to Peterson to discuss the case. "Now let's get down to business. Dr. Lutz, your internist, has asked me to see you regarding that aneurysm of yours. Has he talked to you about it?"
"Vaguely. He said I needed to see you because you're the expert on these things," Peterson answered.
"There's no doubt that I'm the expert," Harshberg said. "Now, I'm going to talk to you about aortic aneurysms in general. I apologize in advance if I repeat things that you already know," he said. As usual, Harshberg went out of his way to be polite during the recruiting session. "An aneurysm is a weak spot in the aorta, the big blood vessel in your belly. It forms something like a balloon. It tends to run in families,

especially on the mother's side. Do you know of anyone in your family with an aneurysm?"

"Not that I am aware of," Peterson said.

"Well, you don't have to have someone in your family with it. You have it and that's all that matters." Harshberg paused to gather his thoughts. "Now, we know by experience that these damn things continue to get bigger with time. No one knows how fast they grow. It's different with different patients. But one thing we know for sure, is that once they reach five centimeters in size, they can burst. The bigger the aneurysm, the higher the chance of it happening..."

Peterson's eyes widened. "What happens when it busts?"

Harshberg knew the patient was now at his mercy. "The majority of people die. Of the lucky ones who make it to the emergency room alive, over half die in the hospital."

"I see."

"Now, there are a lot of people with aneurysms smaller than five centimeters, and they can be left alone, without jeopardizing a person's health. The ones we fix are the ones bigger than five centimeters."

"How big is mine?"

The recruiting session was progressing as planned. "Look here," Harshberg said, pointing to the CAT scan mounted on the light box next to him. "These are the pictures that the radiologist took of your belly. To give you an idea of what we're looking at here, just imagine that you're laying flat on your back, with your head on my table and your feet in the next room. Can you see this white thing right here?"

"Yes."

"It's your back bone. And these are your kidneys next to it. Between the two of them," he pointed to the middle of the picture, "is your aneurysm. It's a big one. Nine centimeters, at least. It's ripe for surgery. What do you think, Dr. Ungaman?"

Cutter was already salivating at the thought of cutting into another belly. "Definitely. This aneurysm needs to come out. There's no doubt about it."

"So, I need to have it fixed?" Peterson asked, as he reached out to hold his wife's hand.

"Yes, sir, you do. It's the right thing to do."

"Well, how about those balloon things? I heard on the radio the other day, that radiologists can fix the aneurysm with a balloon going through the groin."

BEYOND THE MAGIC SCALPEL • 37

Dr. Harshberg looked at me and smiled. "That's what I heard, too. But it's all experimental. Dr. Baldi here is going into interventional and vascular radiology next year. People like him would like to put surgeons like me out of business. But what they do is experimental and I highly advise my patients against it."

"Is this an emergency? How soon does it have to be fixed?" Mrs. Peterson inquired.

"It's not. But the sooner we take care of it the better. Whatever date is convenient for you," Harshberg said.

"Like how soon?" she asked again.

"How about in two days? We have an opening at that time," Cutter noted.

"Suppose I don't have the operation. Do you think that my aneurysm will bust?" Peterson asked.

"The question is not whether it will or not, because it will. The question is not whether you die or not, because you will. The question is simply, when," Harshberg said.

"In two days?" Mr. Peterson mumbled to himself.

"You're scheduled!" Dr. Ungaman jumped in, before Peterson could back out.

"Since we all agree on this, it's my responsibility to inform you of the risks associated with your operation. It's a big surgery and although I do it routinely, I occasionally run into a few complications. You need to be aware of them. You may die, you may suffer a heart attack or a stroke, you may become paralyzed from the waist down, your kidneys may fail, your back may hurt for the rest of your life, and most likely you'll become impotent because of the size of your aneurysm and its location."

"Impotent?" asked the wife.

"One more thing," he continued ignoring her concern. "Your chart says that you've been on the blood thinner, coumadin. I want you to stop taking it and we'll bring you into the hospital tonight and thin your blood with another medicine called heparin."

"Won't that increase my chances for having a stroke? Dr. Lutz said that my blood should be thinned all the time because of my heart valve. He said if it's not, I may get a blood clot from my heart to go to my brain."

"We will make sure that it doesn't happen," Harshberg said, confidently.

"Are you sure that I'll survive all of this?"

"Yes, sir, you will. We have confidence in you," Harshberg said, patting Peterson on the shoulder as he got up. "It was nice meeting the both of you," he added, on his way out. "I'll leave you with Dr. Baldi. He'll take care of some paper work for you and make a few phone calls."

Peterson's decision to opt for surgery was an example of Dr. Harshberg's outstanding recruiting skills. Even the best used car salesman couldn't match his convincing skills.

"How many of these operations has Dr. Harshberg done?" asked Mrs. Peterson as soon as he left the room. "He looks young."

"About seventy a year," I said, as I reached for the consent form her husband needed to sign.

Peterson stared at the form for several minutes before signing reluctantly at his wife's urging.

- Ten -

"Cutter, are you ready to clamp this man's aorta?" Harshberg asked, pointing at Peterson's open belly.

"Sir, I was born ready. Let's squeeze this hard piece of shit," Cutter said, holding the calcified aneurysm in his left hand and reaching for the big metallic clamp with his right.

"Rock and roll, babe," Harshberg said, giving his green light.

"Wait," I exclaimed. "Look at his blood pressure."

"WHAT THE FUCK?" Harshberg shouted. "Why is his pressure so low? Anesthesia, what's going on up there?"

Harshberg always blamed operating room complications on the anesthesia team.

"I'm giving him fluids," the nurse anesthetist said. "Give me a minute or two and his pressure will go back up."

"This is not what I wanted to hear, anesthesia," Harshberg said, in a pissed off voice. "I'm ready to clamp his aorta and you're dicking around up there, not knowing a thing about what you're supposed to be doing." He turned around, looked at Ron, and yelled "WHERE IS THE FUCKIN' ANESTHESIOLOGIST?"

"He's on break," Ron mumbled.

"Get his ass in the room right now," Harshberg ordered. "Where in the fuck does he think he is? Kindergarten? The guy takes a break every half an hour. Rastus, I hate those goddamn anesthesiologists. When you don't need them, there are five of them in the room. When you need them, they're all swarming around a box of doughnuts in the recovery room. The life of Mr. Peterson is in our hands and their hands are fighting for those morning doughnuts that attract them like bugs to a light."

Two minutes later, Gastein rushed into the room.

"Well, it's about time," Harshberg barked. "Dr. Gastein, these aneurysm operations aren't hernia repairs. I can't do them with a nurse anesthetist. I need an anesthesiologist in the room, damn it. It takes less time for this man to bleed to death than it takes you to swallow your doughnut. Fix his FUCKIN' pressure, will you?"

Gastein hated Harshberg's condescending tone, but there wasn't anything he could do about it. Harshberg controlled the operating room because he was the one who was ultimately responsible for the patient's life. That gave him full authority to give shit to anyone he wished.

Once the patient's pressure was back to normal, Harshberg reached for the scalpel. With lightening-quick speed, he cut the aneurysm to reveal its fatty calcified content. Harshberg scooped the brownish-colored stuff out with his hand and held it up in the air to show everybody in the room. It was the shape of a small coconut.

He handed it to Inger. "Save it for Dr. Baldi," he said. "He's having a party this weekend and it will make a great party snack."

"You always make fun of me," I protested.

"What are you trying to say, Rastus?"

"I can't work under such abusive conditions all the time," I cried out.

"Oh, yeah!" Harshberg laughed. "The exit is to your right, son. Go ahead. Don't let the door hit you in the ass on the way out!"

Cutter turned the conversation back to the surgery at hand. "The rest of his aorta is hard like a rock. How in the hell are we going to sew in the graft?" he asked.

"That's the challenge, Cutter. This man doesn't have an aorta anymore. We'll gift him a new one, just like God gave him his first," Harshberg replied. "So, Dr. Baldi, you want to repair these aneurysms with your balloon thing?" He shook his head. "Fuckin' radiologists! You don't know a thing about surgery."

I had to fight back. "That's what you think because you're totally ignorant about developing technologies. A few years ago, surgeons were the only ones draining abscesses and cutting out cancer. Now, the radiologists are doing most of these operations with the help of their machines and new advanced devices," I said. "Things are changing and the future is coming whether you like it or not."

Harshberg frowned, then said, "you, radiologists, are corrupting the medical system. You're ruining it financially."

I didn't take it personally since he hated other specialists, including anesthesiologists, neurologists, and pediatricians. But radiologists were his sore point, because they were quickly encroaching upon the surgeons' territory.

"I stand in the operating room for several hours a day trying to save people's life," Harshberg said. "The radiologist, who's sitting on his ass downstairs, makes more money than I do. It's a rotten medical system."

"You forget, sir, that radiologists are changing the way modern medicine is being practiced," I pointed out. "They get paid a lot of money but they deserve it. If you're upset about your pay, sir, why don't you give up surgery and become a radiologist?"

"Me? Become a radiologist?" he said in disbelief. "Little Rastus is telling Willie Harshberg, chief of cardiovascular surgery at the ACLS, to quit his job as a surgeon and become a radiologist! Did you hear that?" he said as he looked at Inger. "What has the world come to?" He paused for a second and then turned to face me. "SON, I WOULD RATHER TURN GAY BEFORE I WOULD EVEN CONSIDER BECOMING A RADIOLOGIST!"

Harshberg elbowed me to the side. "Someone needs to save this man's life and it sure ain't a radiologist who's going to do it. So, just move out of the way."

Cutter motioned me to his side. "You'll have a better view of the action over here," he said.

After an hour of intense work, Harshberg had repaired Mr. Peterson's aorta. Although he wasn't satisfied with the way the graft was sewn, he decided to call it quits anyway.

"That's the best I can do for him," Harshberg said. "Do you see anymore bleeding, Cutter?"

"No, sir. The field is dry."

"Rastus, go ahead and close his belly. And remember he has an artificial valve sitting in his heart. Thin his blood as soon as he lands in intensive care. I don't want anymore strokes on my service. Is that understood?"

"Yes, sir," I said, unable to hide my excitement. This was the first time Harshberg had personally asked me to close a belly. I suspected it was a subversive decision on his part. He wanted to get me addicted to the knife and hopefully sway me to be a surgeon rather than a radiologist.

"Speaking of stroke," Harshberg continued, "why is Mr. Evans still in the hospital?"

"He's been here for a week already but his progress has been slow," Cutter replied.

"Is his leg healing, Rastus?"

"Yes, sir."

"Then he doesn't need to be on our service. Ship his ass to an extended care facility today," Harshberg said, as he left the operating room.

"Cutter, half of the man's body is still paralyzed. The physical therapist is seeing him," I complained.

"I don't wanna hear it, Mick. I don't call the shots around here. You heard what the boss said. Ship his ass out today."

"Okay," I said, feeling defeated.

"Brother Rastus, you're learning. Just go with the flow. Inger, PDS sutures and tooth forceps to my friend, Dr. Baldi."

"Here you go, doctor," Inger smiled, as she handed them to me.

"Rastus, what's my motto for closing bellies?" Cutter asked.

"A centimeter in and a centimeter down. NO HERNIAS ALLOWED ON THIS SERVICE!" I quickly replied.

"You're learning fast, brother. Keep those stitches tight."

When the operation was over, Cutter asked me not to page him unless a patient was on the verge of death. Tonight was his wife's birthday and he'd promised her a night on the town.

- Eleven -

The hardest part of internship was being woken up frequently during the middle of the night. I hated hearing the ring of a phone or the high-pitched beep of a pager. Even worse, was the voice of a hostile and unpleasant nurse on the telephone, harassing me about some obscure order or telling me about some meaningless, non-urgent medical facts. Suffice it to say, late night calls were rarely pleasant.

"I'm sorry to wake you up, doctor," the hospital operator said. "I have Kari, the nurse from intensive care, on the other line."
"Put her through."
I reached for my bedside lamp and turned it on. It was one thirty in the morning.
"Dr. Baldi," said the voice on the other line. Although I hadn't met Kari, I was already attracted to her soft, friendly, sexy voice, a rarity in the night shift nursing kingdom. That and my loneliness as an intern, set me off on the road to fantasy land whenever I heard her voice.
"It's about Mr. Peterson. His pressure has dropped."
"Give him some fluids."
"I already did."
"How much?"
"One liter."
"Give him more. He's probably still dry from his operation."
"I'm afraid something else might be going on with him," she said, in a concerned voice.
"Like what?"
"Bleeding?"
"Why do you think that?"
"Well, aren't you thinning his blood with heparin?"
"Oh, shit. You're right. Just turn off his heparin and give him more fluids."
"I turned it off about two hours ago but I think he's still bleeding."
"Call the blood bank and order six units of blood in case he needs them. Hopefully he won't. Call me if things change."
"Doctor, are you still there?"
"Yeah."

"I have a bad feeling about all of this."
"What are you trying to say?"
"I'm uncomfortable being with him on my own. I'd prefer it if you were at his bedside."
"You want me there?" I asked, incredulously. I felt wanted by someone. That was a feeling I hadn't had for a while.
"I hate to get you out of bed. But do you mind?"
Of course I minded getting out of my warm bed. But I didn't mind meeting her in the middle of the night.
"Not at all. Give me ten minutes and I'll be there."

When I walked into Peterson's room, Kari was covering his forehead with a cold towel. Her straight, long, blonde hair draped the side of her face. Her pink surgical scrubs were so tight, it was hard not to notice her round, muscular ass and well endowed chest.
"Kari?"
She turned around and smiled. "Thank you for coming."
"How is he doing?"
"Not too well. He hasn't put out any urine for the last three hours. I called the blood bank. His blood units should be here any minute now."
"Good. Very good," I said, in a distracted tone.
It was hard to keep the conversation focused on medicine when Kari was looking at me with her beautiful green eyes. She was absolutely adorable. Everything about her was perfect: her physical look, the way she handled herself, the way she spoke, and the caring manner she expressed towards Mr. Peterson.
"Is this his second liter of fluids?" I finally managed to ask.
"Yes, it is."
"What are you thinking, doctor?" she asked, apparently noticing that my full attention wasn't on the patient.
"Nice. Very nice!" I repeated.
"I beg your pardon?" she asked.
"... I meant, nice work. You've done well stabilizing him so far."
"Thank you."
"Have you been working here for a long time?"
"Three months."
"Where did you work before you came here?" I asked. I wanted to know everything about her.
"Valley Medical," she replied curtly.

"Where did you go to nursing school?"
"Arizona."
"Arizona? Beautiful state. The Grand Canyon, Sedona, Flagstaff... I heard there are some pretty women out there. Is it true?"
"It is a beautiful state, doctor. Now if you excuse me," she said, as she passed by me and headed for the nursing station.
I felt ignored. "Mr. Peterson, how are you doing?" I asked as I laid my hand on his belly and tried to wake him up.
"Hmmm?"
"How are you doing, sir?"
"Fine, I guess."
"Are you having any pain?"
"No pain, doctor. Just heart burns," he replied, pointing to his belly. "Can I have some Maalox?"
I smiled. Poor fellow. He didn't have a clue about what was going on. His perception was distorted by the pain killers he was taking. "Do you get heart burns often?"
Before he could answer, he was already snoring.
"What do you think about his pressure?" Kari inquired.
"Low, but acceptable. Is the blood here, yet?"
"No."
"Give him another liter of fluids."
"Don't you think he needs to go to the operating room?" Kari asked.
I liked her assertiveness.
"He does. But I don't think he's ready to go yet," I said, calmly
"Most doctors would have taken him back to the operating room by now," Kari said, challenging my opinion once again.
I played it cool, though I was beginning to have doubts about my decision. "I can't speak for other doctors," I replied. "But he's my patient, and he'll go to the operating room when I think he's ready."
Kari wasn't backing down. "I'm really uncomfortable taking care of him under the current circumstances," she shot back. "Please do something," she pleaded.
"Trust me," I said. "Time is still on our side."
She wasn't buying it. "If you don't do something about it now, then I will," she said, as she exited the room.
"Where are you going?" I inquired. By now I could tell Kari wasn't one to bluff.

"I'm going to call Dr. Harshberg. This man needs to go to the operating room."

She began to dial, but I grabbed the telephone out of her hand and hung up.

"What do you think you're doing, doctor?" she said angrily.

"I'm trying to save you time, effort, and a bit of humiliation."

"Who do you think you are? My guardian angel?" she asked, sarcastically.

"Don't waste your time trying to get through to Dr. Harshberg. The hospital operator will just refer you back to me. I'm the Harshberg service tonight," I said, in a triumphant tone.

"Then you call him," she demanded.

"Kari, since when do nurses decide that patients need to go to the operating room?" I asked, trying to make my voice as sweet as possible so as not to offend her.

"Look, he's bleeding and he needs help. I think this case is pretty clear cut," she responded.

"Kari, he still hasn't crossed the line."

"What line, doctor?"

"The line that tells me when I need to call Dr. Harshberg in the middle of the night. You know, we interns have a set of rules that help us survive. We want to keep our patients alive but also minimize the number of times we get our ass chewed by our seniors. If I call Harshberg right now, the first thing he's going to ask me is how much fluids and blood we've given Mr. Peterson."

"Three liters of fluids," she hurried to reply.

"That's exactly the point. If I tell him that, he would curse me and hang up the phone."

"Then at what point would you call him?"

"It varies from patient to patient," I said. "For Peterson, the magic number is four liters of fluids and four units of blood," I confidently responded, mentioning arbitrary numbers that just came to my mind.

"But he might die before then," she responded, frantically.

"Bull! Mr. Peterson is a tough man. And besides, people don't die on the Harshberg service. We save lives on this service. You and I will see him through the night. You'll see."

I sat at the desk and watched her keep busy taking care of Mr. Peterson. She hung more fluid and blood units. My loneliness drew me closer to her, although I knew that of all the people in the world, I was the last one she would ever consider for some affection, especially after our heated discussion. So I fantasized about her, about the kind of happiness she could offer me. I imagined her tender caresses.

I dreamt about her as she stood a few feet away from me. I envied Mr. Peterson, the current recipient of her tender care and devoted attention...

- Twelve -

Harshberg and Cutter arrived in the intensive care unit at six-thirty in the morning to check on Mr. Peterson.

"His belly looks like a pregnant woman ready to deliver. What in the fuck did you do to him, son?" Harshberg asked me.

"Sir, he bled most of the night. It all went into his belly. His pressure dropped a few times but he responded well to fluids. We've given him four units so far. And we turned off his heparin as soon as he started bleeding."

"I was afraid that was going to happen," Harshberg said. "His aortic valve made me nervous. I'm surprised you were able to keep him alive."

"I tried my best, sir," I responded, then looked at Kari.

"How much heparin did you give him after the operating room?"

I could tell Cutter was hoping that I hadn't fucked up.

"On arrival I gave him ten thousand units of heparin and started him on an infusion of a thousand per hour..."

Harshberg's jaw dropped. "Rastus, don't tell me that I heard you right. How much did you give him?" he asked again.

"Ten thousand units and an infusion of one..."

Before I could finish my sentence, he jumped in. "Who in the fuck told you to do that?" he barked.

"Siiir... I thought that you asked me to fully thin his blood."

"I did. But who told you to give him ten thousand units?" He was pissed.

"The Duke surgical manual. Supposedly, they have the best intensive care in the country," I replied, unable to hide the tremor in my voice.

"Where's the fuckin' manual?"

"Right here, sir," I said, pulling the small book out of my pocket.

"Show me the page." He extended his right arm and waited for me to hand him the book.

"Right here, sir. It says ten to twenty thousand units for thromboembolic events."

"BUT NOT FOR STROKE PREVENTION!" he yelled. "You knifed the inside of this man. We need to open him up again." He looked at Cutter. "Shit, that's all I needed on my clinic day.

Cutter, go to clinic and start recruiting. Rastus and I will take him back."

"Yes, sir."

"Rastus, I'll meet you in the OR," he snapped. "Get him transported right away."

"Yes, sir."

Kari, who was stone-faced during the entire conversation, grinned.

"Let's go, anesthesia. NO TIME FOR DOUGHNUTS THIS MORNING," yelled Dr. Harshberg inside OR seven. "Let's move it, people. I have a few dozen patients I need to see in clinic today."

"We're doing the best we can," Gastein replied.

"I guess your best ain't fast enough. Move it, Gastein," he ordered.

I watched silently as Harshberg stood on the opposite side of the operating table with his arms crossed.

"Go ahead, Rastus. Remove the staples," he said in a surprisingly soft tone.

Frantically, I started picking up the metallic staples embedded in Mr. Peterson's skin. My hands were shaking.

He stood and watched for awhile. "Knife," Harshberg demanded, as he assumed his position at the table. He grabbed the scalpel from Inger, pushed my hands out of the way and quickly cut open Mr. Peterson's belly, which was drenched in blood. "Don't stand there like a statue, Rastus. Grab that sucker and suck up all the mess you made," he finally ordered.

I tried to suction the blood as fast as I could so that Harshberg could see what he was doing. He pushed the intestines to one side and exposed the graft he had sewn the previous day. "What the hell. Let me stitch the graft one more time," he said. "Do you see any bleeding, son?"

"No, sir."

"Ten thousand units. Ten fucking thousand units! You know, Rastus, you're more dangerous than I thought," he said, trying to provoke me.

"I'm awfully sorry, sir," I replied.

"Let this be a lesson to you," he added, in a professorial tone. "That pen in your pocket can kill patients. All it takes is one wrong order and the patient is history."

"From now on, I'll think twice before writing anything," I promised.

Harshberg wanted me to squirm some more so he continued with his interrogation. "Do you feel bad about it?" he asked.

"Yes, sir, I do," I replied.

"I do, too. Very bad. Do you know why I feel so bad, Rastus?"

"Why, sir?"

"Because I didn't fry your ass in front of the nursing staff this morning. How could I have missed such an opportunity?" he joked.

"Sir, you should have. But not because of the heparin," I thoughtlessly replied.

"Why then?"

"Sir, I was preoccupied with Mr. Peterson's nurse," I replied reluctantly.

"Kari?"

I smiled nervously. "Yes, sir. I think there's a good chance for some romance," I said, winking my right eye.

Harshberg was amused. "Did you hear that? My patient was bleeding to death and my intern was trying to screw his nurse!" he said to Inger. "I guess it's understandable. Rastus, like most male interns, is suffering from a serious illness."

"What illness?" inquired the anesthesiologist.

"The surgical intern syndrome: hornitis! They're horny all the time, hypersexual, hungry, sleepy, and they never remember anything we teach them!"

"It's hard being the intern, sir. It gets lonely at times."

"Yes, it does. But your priority should be your education. Don't make screwing nurses your hobby," he smiled. "Then again, you Mediterranean boys have so much testosterone in your blood, you need dialysis to take some off," he laughed.

"Can't act against my genes, sir," I joked as I watched him sew the graft a second time.

Harshberg could never leave the operating room without giving some last words of advice. "Just remember, son, that penis of yours... I meant that pen of yours, can kill patients. Be careful how you use it next time!"

"Gently and with great care, sir," I smirked.

I'd finally managed to gain Harshberg's respect. And it wasn't my surgical prowess that did it!

- Thirteen -

In the clinic, Harshberg always paraded the hallways escorted by his chief resident and intern. He enjoyed the image of power, control and toughness.
"Here come the surgeons. Step to the side and bow down," Dr. Lutz said as he gently pushed his resident to clear the way.
"Better watch out!" Harshberg shot back. "When was the last time you ate, Dr. Lutz?"
Harshberg hated the internist.
"Last night," Lutz replied.
"Cutter, put him on the schedule for today," Harshberg joked.
"But I don't need an operation!" Lutz replied nervously.
"Of course, you do. We all do. The question is when and what kind of an operation," Harshberg teased.
"Speaking of operation, did Mr. Peterson get his already?" Lutz inquired.
"He had an aneurysm the size of a monkey's head. We got the sucker out yesterday."
"Hopefully, you helped him," Lutz said sarcastically.
"No, my friend. I didn't help him, I cured him. You, internists, give patients pills and try to help them. We, surgeons, cut them and cure them. Your patient is cured, Dr. Lutz. You can rest assured," he replied with a cynical smile.
"It's all relative, all a matter of opinion," the internist fought back.
"All a matter of reality. A pill is fake. A knife is real. Never underestimate the power of a knife, Lutz. A chance to cut is always a chance to cure." He turned around and looked at Cutter and me. "Let's go, boys. I can't waste anymore time when I have all these people waiting for me to cut and cure them."
"A scalpel does magic!" Cutter said as we hurried down the hallway.
When we reached the end, Harshberg commented, "Rastus, I hate those goddamn internists. They're a lazy species of doctors. Take our work, for example. We, surgeons, work hard to save people's lives and cure them from ugly diseases. They, on the other hand, mentally masturbate all day while

entertaining a variety of insignificant topics. They like to hold hands and do shit of the sort."

"What a boring job they have," Cutter added.

"Boring, indeed. You just couldn't pay me enough to do what they do. Besides, our philosophy is different," he continued as we resumed walking. "I just hate the fuckers!"

Cutter's obnoxious laugh could be heard at the other end of the hallway.

"CUTTER!" cried Harshberg.

"SIR?" he snapped to attention and quit laughing.

"Who do we see next?"

"Two patients in the next hallway, Mrs. Jones and Mr. Merck," he answered.

"Why are we seeing them?"

"Jones needs her breast removed. Merck needs a new foot."

"I remember Jones now. She's another one of Lutz' patient, one he couldn't cure with his useless pills," he said smiling. "But who's Merck? How come you haven't told me a thing about him?"

"Sir, I intended to..."

Harshberg hated the word *intended*. "Intentions don't count for shit! How many times do I have to tell you that?"

"No excuse, sir."

"That's what I wanna hear. Go see Jones and schedule her for whatever she wants done. Call Lutz afterwards and tell him what you two have decided."

"Sir, she requested to see you personally..."

"Cutter, you know that I have no interest in a sick breast. Rastus, the only breast I'm interested in is the one I see in bed, if you know what I mean," he smiled, as he winked his right eye and tilted his cowboy hat.

"So... I see her by myself?" Cutter tried to clarify.

"Do just like I told you."

"Yes, sir. Consider it done." No one could follow orders as well as Cutter.

"Good. Rastus, come with me. Let's go see this new character, Merck. Where is he, anyhow?"

"Room twenty-one. He's been waiting for two hours," informed Cutter.

"As if I care how long he's been waiting!"

When we entered the room, Merck was already sitting on the examining table, stripped down to his underwear.

"Good afternoon, Mr. Merck. I'm Dr. Harshberg from cardiovascular surgery. This is my assistant, Dr. Baldi."

"Doctor who?" he asked, pointing at me.

"Dr. Baldi," repeated Harshberg.

"Baldi? Baldi like in bald?" he asked, looking at my head.

"Baldi like in Italian," I hurried to counter his offensive comment.

Harshberg stepped in. "Why are you undressed?"

"The nurse asked me to. She said I need to be examined."

"I'm a surgeon, not an internist. I don't examine patients, I only cut them."

It was true. Harshberg never cared to examine his patients.

"Don't you want to look at it?" he asked pointing to his gangrenous right foot.

"I already saw it. Now please get up and put your clothes back on," he continued, as he sat at the desk.

"That quickly?"

"Mr. Merck, please get up and put your clothes back on unless you want to walk naked around the clinic!" he exclaimed impatiently.

He got up and started getting dressed. "Doc, my foot is killing me. My life has been a nightmare lately. I just can't take it anymore. Can you help me?"

Harshberg was busy looking through the chart.

"Some days I wonder about what's happening to me. I don't deserve this mess..."

"Your foot is rotten because of the gangrene. You have no blood supply down there," he said as he pointed at it. "You would be better off without it."

"You mean cut it off?"

"Yes, I mean a nice, clean amputation. Do you have a problem with that?" he replied looking at him with his sharp eyes.

"It's my foot and I would rather die before seeing it come off."

"I know it's a hard thing to accept," Harshberg said with a soft voice, "but I'm afraid it may be your only option."

"Only option? I came to you because they told me you were the best. They said that you operate on people that everyone else had given up on. Can't you do something for me?" he begged him.

"I'm afraid not. Not at your stage."

"With all the modern technology and all these fancy operations I see on the television and there's nothing you can do for me?" he said in disbelief.

"Mr. Merck, there is a lot I can do for you. As a matter of fact, I can cut you in anyway I want. But this is not the question. In your case, the question is, what should I do. I would look awfully stupid if I killed you while trying to pick on your foot to fix its blood supply. You have a problem, Mr. Merck."

"I know I have a problem. That's why I came to see you."

"Your heart is thrashed, at least that's what the cardiologist thinks. These Marlboros," he said, pointing to the cigarettes in Mr. Merck's shirt, "haven't done you any favor. The arteries of your body are all clogged up, including those going to your heart and legs. I'm afraid that your heart wouldn't tolerate a big operation like the one I would have to do to save that leg of yours. You may lose your life."

"I can't believe what I'm hearing. I came to you hoping to find a surgeon who can do the job. Aren't you surgeons supposed to save people from death?" He knew how to target Harshberg's weak spot and challenge his ego.

"Yes, I'm a surgeon. And yes, I'm supposed to save people from death. I do compete against the devil frequently. I try to beat him and get my patients out of the grave before he lays his hand on them. Sometimes I succeed. Or may I say, he let's me win. But who am I fooling? When the prince of darkness wants to win, he always does. Satan is a tough man to deal with."

Mr. Merck ignored the last comment. "I thought I came to the best. Maybe I didn't after all." It was meant as a blow to Harshberg's ego. Mr. Merck knew what he was doing. "I guess I should leave," he said as he got up to go.

"Sit down, Mr. Merck. I'm not quite done with you, yet," he ordered him. "Your heart is bad. If I don't operate, your leg will get infected, and you'll die. If I do operate, I may kill you on the table. Either way we look at it, there's no way out for you." He sounded firm but sincere.

Merck thought for a few seconds. "If I'm going to die, I would much rather die in your operating room than watch my foot rot. Do you have enough courage to do the job or should I go find a surgeon who does?"

I looked at Harshberg. Under most circumstances, he would have lost his patience, especially since his ego was under attack. But he sat there and thought about the whole situation. For one reason or another, he seemed to care about Merck. I didn't know why.

"Do you really understand what I'm trying to tell you here?" he asked.

"Yes, I do. I accept the risk of the operation. I want it. Do you think that you can help me?"

Harshberg hesitated for a little bit. "Let me speak with the cardiologist and see what we can do for you. Dr. Baldi will stay here with you and tentatively schedule you for the operating room next week. I don't know what type of operation we'll do. Give me some time to think about it," he said as he got up and extended his right hand for a shake. "No matter what happens, Mr. Merck, I wish you luck."

Mr. Merck sat in silence as I filled out his paper work and made a few phone calls. Occasionally, he looked up at the ceiling.

"Okay. You need to sign your name right here," I said, as I put the form in front of him on the table.

"What was your name again?" he asked.

"Dr. Mick Baldi."

"Dr. Baldi, are you going bald?"

"I beg your pardon?"

"I'm sorry I asked. It's none of my business," he apologized. "Do I have to sign this form?"

"Yes, sir, you do. It's required by law before we do anything to you."

"Am I signing my life away to Dr. Harshberg?"

"No, sir. You're giving him permission to do your operation." I tried to maintain my professionalism.

He pulled a small bottle out of his pocket after he signed. "I see. Can you refill my ulcer medication?"

"I'll be happy to." I grabbed the prescription pad out of the drawer and wrote him a month's worth of supply.

"I just need two weeks."

"You're a smoker. You need it for at least one month."

"Just two weeks, doc. I'll be gone by then."

"Gone where?"

"Visiting Satan," he replied, with a wicked smile.

There was something strange about Mr. Merck. "I don't know if you'll be or not. I guess we'll have to wait and see," I said.

"Come on, doc, be honest with me. You know it's over. Isn't that why Dr. Harshberg doesn't want to touch me? Isn't why he wished me good luck?"

"He wants the best for you, sir."

Merck rubbed his head and looked down at the floor. "Satan, buddy, I'm finally coming to visit you."

I thought the man had gone crazy. "Please, Mr. Merck. Calm down. You're not dead, yet."

"You seem so confident. Can you guarantee that I'll be alive in two weeks?"

"No. But I can't guarantee that you'll be dead either. Only time will tell, Mr. Merck."

- Fourteen -

"Qui crepitat vivat!"
(Who farts, lives!)

Bowel movements are a fact of life, one that's hard to forget about in hospital settings. For the elderly patients at the ACLS, bowel movements were their top priority. Some could talk for fifteen minutes straight about the color, consistency of their bowel movements on a particular day and about their gut activity for the last thirty years!

Why are bowel movements so important in surgery? For the surgeons, passing gas and having a bowel movement after an operation are reliable signs of bowel recovery. For patients, they are the only ticket for a hot meal after a long period of starvation. For the poor interns, such as myself, they are the main prerequisite for discharging the patient out of the hospital. It's in everybody's best interest when a patient passes gas: surgeons are reassured, patients are happily fed and interns get some sleep!

The day I met Mr. Merck, I concluded my evening bowel rounds at the bedside of Mr. Peterson. I was anxious to see him after his second trip to the operating room earlier that day --going under the knife twice in such a short period of time was a dangerous activity, especially for someone his age.

To my pleasant surprise, he seemed in pretty good shape considering everything he had gone through.

"Do you know who's taking care of Mr. Peterson tonight?" I asked the unit secretary after visiting with him.

"I am," Kari said from behind me.

I was happy to see her again. "Hi, Kari. Peterson seems to have done well today, don't you think?"

"Yeah. That's what the day nurse told me. No bleeding so far."

"That's good."

"Any special instructions for tonight?" she asked me.

"No, just call me if you need me. I think he'll be all right. He couldn't be in better hands than yours," I replied smiling.

Her face lit up with satisfaction. "Thanks you for your vote of confidence."

"Well, I guess I better get going. Good night."

"Good night, doctor... Oh, before you leave, I just wanted to let you know that I thought about you today."

My heart skipped a beat. Thought about me? In what way?

"Last night it was stressful for me. I'm sure that it was for you, too. But I think you handled it well as a first year doc."

I was flattered.

"Thanks, Kari. It's nice to hear a positive thing every now and then."

Emboldened by her compliment, I decided to ask her out.

"Can you please come into Mr. Peterson's room?" I wanted to avoid the potential gossip by the unit secretary.

Intrigued by my request, she followed me into Peterson's room. He was snoring. "Kari, I meant to ask you something..."

"What do you need?"

"I've been wondering about something... Uuuh, what are the chances that you and I have coffee together one of these evenings?"

Her face turned serious. "Very slim..."

I didn't let her finish. "I understand. You don't have to explain further. I'm sorry I asked."

She looked at me and smiled. "Very slim the next couple of days because I'm working evenings. But I have next week off."

I was speechless.

"So doctor, are you going to ask me out or were you just wondering about it?"

Up to that moment, internship had been the worst experience of my life. Still recovering from a lost love, stressed and constantly harassed by Willie Harshberg and some of his crazy patients and nurses, the thought of holding Kari in my arms gave my life a whole new meaning and opened a new chapter in my internship.

- Fifteen -

For five days and nights, I obsessed over Kari. I thought about her as often as I could and dreamt of what it would be like to sit with her in a romantic coffee shop, sipping some Colombian coffee while admiring her beauty. She had all the ingredients necessary to make a man happy: a gorgeous figure, a winsome personality and smarts. Her warm smile conquered my heart, and I was determined to seduce her at any cost.

Our date was scheduled for Sunday night. I sat by the window and waited for her to pick me up. She was five minutes late. When her car lights approached the driveway, I hurried outside to meet her.

"Are you going to get in or are you just going to stand there?" she asked, as she sat behind the steering wheel of a shiny, red 1965 convertible Corvette.

"Man, I knew that intensive care nurses made big money but I wasn't expecting this," I said, admiring her car.

"My father gave it to me for my eighteenth birthday. Do you like it?"

"Do I like it?" I said, shaking my head. "Of course, I do. What kind of a father do you have?"

"He's a wealthy cardiologist."

"Lucky you."

"Come on. Let's go," she said.

"I'm not sure I can afford to pay for the ride," I teased her.

"The ride is free, doctor. But you may have to pay for the rest!"

"Please call me Mick, or Rastus, if you wish."

"Okay, Mick the doc. Get in and that's an order," she said winking her right eye.

"YES, MA'AM. I like to follow orders," I replied, as I jumped into the passenger seat. "This is the best treat I've had in a long time."

"Where do you wanna go?"

"I don't care. As long as I go with you in this car."

"Like some music?" she said, as she leaned forward and turned on the radio. "How about this?"

"Great choice. I haven't heard this song for ages." Joe Cocker sang *unchain my heart, please set it free.*

"He's good."

"I spent my college years listening to Joe Cocker. He's the best," I continued.

"Is this your favorite song of his?"

"*Unchain My Cock*... Sorry, I meant *Unchain My Heart*?"

"You, men!"

"I'm really sorry. I had no intention of offending you. We used to always sing that in college. To get back to your question, yes, it's my favorite."

"Well then, we have something in common," she smiled.

"Kari, has your heart been chained before?" I asked, as we approached the freeway entrance.

She answered a question with a question. "Mick, do you believe in love?"

"Love?"

"Yeah. Do you think love exists?"

"It depends on who you ask," I replied. "If you ask a poet, for example, it does."

"How about if I ask a doctor?"

"It depends," I said.

I was doing my best to be vague but Kari pressed on. "Do you believe in it?" she asked.

"Does it really matter what I believe?"

"It matters to me," she replied with a sweet, caring voice.

She was putting me on the spot, and the only way I knew how to get out was by cracking a joke. "Sure I believe in love," I said. "I love the weather tonight. God, it's so pleasant out here."

"You've been with the surgeons for too long," she said, in a disappointed tone.

"What do you mean?"

"You guys disconnect yourselves from the reality of the world and isolate yourself to protect your feelings. It's sad, because deep down you have a lot to offer and a lot to gain in return. But for some reason you decide to sacrifice love and feelings.".

"What do you know about love, Kari?"

"Not much. But I'm sure that I know more about it than you have or will ever know in your life time."

She didn't know me at all.

"Look," I told her. "The love I've known may be incomprehensible to you."

"Try me?" she said.

"Not tonight."

"Why not?"
"I have to be at work eight hours from now. It's another one of those twelve-day shifts."
"Then why don't we spend the night together and you can tell me all about it?" she said, nonchalantly.
"But I thought we were going to a cafe?"
"Nope. We're going up to the mountains."
"Is that why you took the freeway?"
"It's not far. Just thirty miles from here," she said, mischievously.
"Did you plan all of this?"
"What if I did?" she hurried to reply. "I thought it would be nice to get to know you. It's such a pleasant night. Look at all the beautiful stars. There's a lake up there. We can sit at the edge of the water, sip some wine and talk."
"I can't believe this is really happening," I grinned. I felt like a kid on his way to a candy store. "Wait, how about work tomorrow?" I asked.
"What time do you have to be at the hospital?"
"Five in the morning."
"I can't promise you any sleep tonight but I can promise to get you to the hospital by five."
Her offer was irresistible.
"Oh, fuck it! What do I have to lose?" I said as I looked at the starry sky and lifted my arms up in the air. "Hey... Where are we going to get the wine?"
"The chilled Chardonay is in the trunk."
"You devil!" I commented, amused by her intricate plans.

- Sixteen -

With a blanket beneath us and another one wrapped around us, Kari and I sat at the edge of the water with a full view of the lake and the mountains surrounding it. Millions of stars lit the sky. Occasionally, one flashed across the sky and disappeared behind the mountains. A full battalion of crickets and squads of frogs played their music in the background. Whenever one of us took a sip of wine, the other watched and giggled. Far away from the rest of the world, Kari and I sat together like two old friends. Nothing else mattered. I was mesmerized by her whispering voice. I was in Heaven.

"Funny how we met," Kari said, after a long silence. "In a way, I'm surprised that we're here together. You were so cocky the first time I met you. To be quite frank, I didn't like you much."

"At least you're honest," I replied.

"But the more I thought about all the things you have to go through as an intern, the more sympathy I felt for you. I can't imagine being in your shoes. You have to please everyone: the consultants, the nurses, the patients, their families..."

"It's hard. But the hardest part of it isn't the stress. It's the loneliness," I said.

"How can a person as busy as you get lonely?"

"People have a lot of misconceptions about doctors. They don't know what we are like when our white coats come off."

"Really?"

"Why do you think we wear white coats?"

"Cleanliness?"

"No, we wear them to conceal our human weaknesses, vices, insecurities, vulnerability, depression, fears and loneliness. People expect us to be healers. So we dress in white coats and present ourselves as healers. Little do they know that we're actors. We perform our act and hope that they get better."

"I never thought about it that way," Kari said.

"No matter how big your audience is, it can get very lonely when you're the actor on stage," I continued, "especially if it's the same act that you're performing over and over again -- taking care of patients. Our days are spent listening to their fears, watching them suffer, saving their lives by poking their bodies with needles, slicing them with knives and mixing their blood with medicines. That's how we act. But do you think we ever tell them about how we truly feel? How scared we are that one day we or someone we love may have to face the same reality that they're facing? The stress, the long hours, and the suffering I see don't bother me. Loneliness and fear does."

Kari reached for the wine. "Here, Mick. Let's make a toast to the healing actors." With her right hand behind my extended neck and her left holding the wine bottle, she poured the wine down my throat.

"I really needed to have a night like this."

"That's why I brought you here. And you know, Mick, you're not alone. I'm lonely too."

"A beautiful woman like you?"

"Yes, a beautiful woman like me. Are you surprised?"

"You can have ten thousand men at your feet anytime you want."

"Ten thousand. Perhaps more. But not one loves me the way I want. So far there hasn't been one who can hold me the way I want to be held."

"You talk like you're heart has been wounded."

"Three times."

"Three times, what?"

"Three husbands."

"You have been married to three men?"

"Yup."

"I thought you were only allowed one husband. Is it legal to marry three?"

"Very funny," she said, pushing me away. "You know what I'm trying to tell you. Are you making fun of me?"

"Come here," I said, as I pulled her toward my chest. "If you want to tell me about it, I promise I'll listen without making any judgments."

"Okay," she said. "At eighteen, I had my first teenage love. When I look back on that time, I realize all the mistakes I made. It didn't take much for him to get my heart. He said a few nice things to me and before I knew it, we were married. We had a fun time together. We explored our blossoming sexuality and had many wild adventures."

"Wild thing," I said. "We all love doing the wild thing..."

"Only the beginning was wild," she said. "After my first pregnancy, things started changing. We had a baby boy and, a year later, a girl. He wasn't ready. I tried the best I could to make my family life a happy one. But we started drifting apart and I took up nursing school to fill the gap in my life."

"Why did you stay with him?"

"Because I didn't believe in divorce at the time."

"And then?"

She grabbed the bottle and drank some more. "I caught him in bed with my best friend... I thought it was my fault. Maybe I wasn't fulfilling his fantasies. We went through a lot of counseling. But apparently he loved too many women."

"So you left him?"

"Of course. Can you imagine sleeping next to someone you love, knowing that only an hour ago he had shared his body with someone else? Can you imagine smelling her scent on his clothes? It was hell. I cried until I ran out of tears and then I threw him out."

"Why would anyone cheat on a beautiful woman like you?"

She looked up at me with her sweet eyes and wept.

"Sorry, Kari. Sorry to hear that you went through all of this." I offered her the sleeve of my sweater to wipe her cheeks.

"After anger and sadness, came depression. I had a lot to deal with. My feelings, my future, but more importantly my children. Can you imagine being a single mom with two kids, having to work full-time?"

Her story made internship seem like smooth-sailing.

"Overall I was better off without him. It was hard, especially on the kids. But I had no other choice. It wasn't my fault."

"What did you do to forget him?"

"Time was my medicine. Two years later, I met a farmer in the hospital. He was visiting his sick mother."

"A farmer?"

"He was a nice man. Not too intelligent but nice, sweet, and very loyal. He worshipped me and followed me around like a little puppy..."

"That's cute!"

"It was, but it didn't last long..."

"Don't tell me you caught him in bed with your friend?"

"No, my poor second husband drowned in a lake one night trying to save one of his friends. I was pregnant with my third baby."

"Jesus! Do you have any luck in life?"

"Sometimes I ask myself the same question," she sulked.

"How about your third husband? Any luck there?"
"Life went on and I always thought that it would be nice to live with someone again. But I didn't make any effort to meet other people. Besides, I had my kids to look after."
"Yeah, I think kids are always a problem," I replied. I tried to imagine how I would handle the situation if I were her third husband.
"One night I was working an extra shift down in the emergency room. It was a very busy night so I went to the cafeteria to grab some coffee. I sat down at one of the tables and started looking at a newspaper someone had left behind. As I was turning the pages, I noticed someone sitting at the table next to me. When I looked up, there was this handsome young paramedic licking an ice cream cone..."
"Licking an ice cream cone? Highly suggestive if you ask me."
"It's true. And I'm sure that if it was anyone else it would have been a complete turn off. But he was really cute and his smile was so innocent. He held his ice cream cone like a kid."
"I see..."
"He was fun to talk to. I invited him to join me and the kids for a picnic. They hit it off from the start and within two months we were married."
"Pretty gutsy!"
"I know. I wasn't thinking at the time..."
"No, I meant gutsy for him. I mean to walk into a family of three kids. No offense but you really have to question the sanity of any man who does that."
"I guess so. But he always said that the sex was awesome. Maybe that's what hooked him."
"I know the feeling. I mean, who wouldn't fall in love with someone like you? Your beauty is like a wicked web."
"Wicked web?"
"Sorry, I'm really getting drunk," I said with my eyes barely opened. "So what happened to him in the end?"
"How do you know there was an end?"
I looked at her eyes. "If there wasn't an end, you wouldn't be sitting here in my arms completely wasted with your eyes crossed!"
"Are my eyes really crossed?"
"Either yours or mine. But someone's eyes are!"
"I wished I had my camera," she replied giggling.
"So what happened to prince charming?"

"Prince charming?"
"Mister paramedic..."
"He suddenly disappeared. I came home one night and he was gone. But all his stuff was still around."
"Did you call the police?"
"They looked everywhere for him. He was declared missing on the television news. A week later they found him."
"Dead?"
"No. He was spending time with another girlfriend fifty miles away from home..."
"Man, you have quite a story there."
"Yes, I do. And the moral of my story is simple: men are shit."
"I feel the same about men, that's why I hate dating them," I kidded.
She hit my flank with her right elbow. "You, men!"
"Ouch. You know I was joking."
"I hate all of you."
"Don't say that."
"I really do."
"Every woman needs a man. And every man needs a woman. We can't live without each other," I said, desperately trying to woo her back in my arms.
"That's not true. Mother Teresa is by herself," she shot back defiantly.
"That's because she's been looking for the right guy all this time. Why do you think she goes traveling around the world?"
"To find the right one?"
"That's right," I replied swinging my head. "The best gift that God can give any of us is a hug and a kiss by someone who loves us. Someone who cares."
"You're drunk, Mick. You're drunk and horny," she said laughing.
"No, I'm not."
"Are you sure?"
"Positive. I wouldn't even care if you were sitting next to me naked right now."
"Oh, really? We'll see how fast you'll change your mind..."

- Seventeen -

Kari was terrific. Listening to her as she sat in my arms made me very happy. I tried to understand why two men walked away and abandoned such a beauty, one so vulnerable to love and romance. I wanted her desperately. But right when I was about to make my move, she said she had to go to the bathroom.

"I feel much better now," she said when she returned. "It's all the wine we've been drinking."

"I wish I could say the same. You gave me blue balls, got up and went to the bushes. It's not fair..." I complained.

"Don't worry, doc. It was only the appetizer."

"You mean it's a whole meal I'm being served tonight?"

"At a class A restaurant!" she joked.

"You better hurry, Chef, because I'm afraid I'll be asleep before you get a chance to serve me the main course..."

"Be patient, Mick. We're trying to get to know each other."

"I know your name, where you live and work, and what kind of a car you drive. I guess it's all I need to know. Can we get to..." I had the hiccups.

"I need to know more about you."

"Like what?" I asked as she sat down and cuddled with me. Our lips met briefly.

"What was that foreign love you talked about earlier?"

"Just like it sounded. Foreign."

"Foreign like what?"

I wanted to get laid. She wanted to talk.

"Foreign like different. Unusual. Dream like."

"Tell me about your foreign love."

"Not tonight, Kari. Maybe some other time."

"Please. I like to hear stories when I am in the arms of a man."

"It's a long story. I'm afraid I can't tell it tonight," I mumbled.

"Why not?"

"Because the wine makes me wanna fuck, not talk!"

"Good reason. But please, Mick, try to tell me about your love."

"Oh, Lord. There must be something better to do right now then tell a story," I said, as I laid on my back to look at the sky.

"Come on, Mick. I opened my heart to you."
"The only love story I've known I've been trying to bury in the past."
"Come on, Mick."
Boy was she stubborn. I finally gave in. "It was the spring of my first year in medical school. My best friend, Greg, and I had just returned from surfing in Santa Cruz. We decided to have a quick beer at one of the local pubs in Palo Alto, the 42nd Street..."
"Where's Palo Alto?"
"In California."
"You went to school there?"
"Yeah, Stanford."
"Smart dude!"
"Right now more horny than smart!" I quipped. "Anyhow, the 42nd street doesn't exist anymore. But back then it was a nice place to go for a drink. We stood on the second floor and looked at the women passing by. I suddenly felt someone tugging on my sweater. I turned around and saw this drunk woman. She wanted me to taste her drink. Just as I was about to take a sip, I noticed one of her six friends. She had a natural look with silky blonde hair and blue eyes..."
"Is that why you're attracted to me? Because I have blonde hair."
"Sort of. But back then I really didn't have a preference. I took women as they came."
"Oh, excuse me, Dr. Stud!"
"Do you wanna hear the story or are you going to keep interrupting me?"
"Go on. Please, go on."
"She wore a black jacket that day. I tried talking to her but she was a bit shy. Part of it was that she didn't speak the language well, or maybe that's how she was. I asked her name. It sounded a little strange and she had to repeat it three times. Finally I asked her to write it on the palm of my hand. Her handwriting was pretty: *Gulla*. Her drunk friend helped her spell it."
"What kind of a name was *Gulla*?"
"European. And she did have the face of a European woman, a pretty one. There was something about her face and innocent look that captured my heart on the spot. I got this overwhelming feeling that she was the woman I wanted to spend the rest of my life with. But it was hard to get her

attention. I didn't think she was interested in me because she left with her friends."

"And then?"

"Greg encouraged me to go after her so I started running and caught up with her just when she was about to reach the door. She was a bit surprised when I tapped her on the shoulder and asked for her telephone number. At first, she refused, but I begged her a few times and she gave it to me. I can't describe to you how happy I was when she agreed to meet me again."

"Then what happened?"

"We met in the courtyard of the Gatehouse, a restaurant that used to be in Palo Alto. I showed up late as usual to find her dressed in a pretty sheep wool sweater. We sat at a table next to the wall and sipped some hot herbal tea. Her innocent smile made my heart ache for her. And every time I saw the reflection of the flickering light on her face, I felt like I was the luckiest man in the world."

"She must have been really special."

"Before we knew it, we were both drifting down the river of love and escaping into a dream world, one filled with fairy tales..."

"I'm really liking this story," she said, as she kissed my neck.

I took another sip of the wine and kept talking. "I was twenty-three years old and this was my first love. For her pretty blue eyes, I was willing to do anything and go anywhere, even across the Atlantic, to Iceland, where she was from. A few days after we met, I dropped her off at the airport. Two months later, I was on my way to Iceland to fetch her back."

"How romantic," Kari said.

"I was nervous," I continued. "I remember watching the break of dawn as the plane approached the ground. The day I die, I think I'm going to see that dawn again. It was the most beautiful thing I ever saw. There was this song playing on one of the flight's radio channels. The singer kept repeating *it must have been love but it's over now, it must have been good...* I thought it was a bad omen. But the minute I saw her at the airport, I had no doubt that she loved me more than anything else in her life."

"What was Iceland like?"

"Paradise. We spent the summer in the western mountains on her family's farm."

"Is it really paradise?"

"If God ever decided to name a paradise on earth, he would chose Iceland. Huge waterfalls, clean rivers, endless meadows and green prairies, unspoiled fields covered with pretty small white and yellow wild flowers, hills covered with blue berries, mountain sheep gazing peacefully, and gorgeous horses running up the hills."

Kari's eyes were closed, as she listened to my descriptions. "What an experience!" she sighed.

"Can you imagine a Viking in love? Gulla had the spirit of one. She loved nature. We spent hours riding horses in the wilderness, fishing trout and salmon, picking berries and staining our tongues and faces with the delicious fruit. We watched many sunsets from the top of lonely volcanoes and made love at the edge of every lake we came across," I said, pausing to ask Kari if it was okay for me to be telling he rest of the story.

"I want you to tell me more," she said.

"Every day we spent together was a dream. Our bodies were glued together and we made love more often than we ate. We were burning with sexual desire and we needed each other so much, that we missed each other even when we were together. Our love grew stronger day by day. Then summer came to an end." I reached for the wine.

"Ever since I was little, I've always hated the end of the summer. Why can't summer last forever?" she asked.

"I don't know. But it never lasts forever. There's always an end."

"What a sad end."

"No, it was just the end of the summer. We couldn't let go of each other..."

Before I finished, Kari pressed her lips against mine.

"Wait, don't you want to hear the end?" I asked.

"Shut up, Mick," she whispered, as she nailed me to the ground and climbed on top of me. Her long hair covered my face. "Shut up and kiss me..."

- Eighteen -

"MICK, MICK, WAKE UP," shouted Kari, as she shook me. "It's six o'clock."
    I opened my eyes and was blinded by the sunrise. "Leave me alone," I said, pulling the blanket over my head.
    "Get up, Mick. We need to go."
    "What's the hurry?" I groaned.
    She shook me again. "You had to be at work an hour ago. Get up."
    "What?"
    "You're late for work. Get up, Mick."
    "Oh, shit!" I exclaimed.

We parked at the back entrance of the hospital at about 7 a.m.. Kari gave me a brief hug. "Bye. I'll see you later."
    "I really don't want to leave you. Can't I stay with you for the day?"
    "Mick, you're acting like a kid. Come on, get out and go. You're two hours late already."
    "I never finished telling you the story."
    "I want to hear it, but not now. Go, Mick. Go," she replied, as she leaned towards me and opened the passenger door.
    "It was wonderful. Just wonderful," I said on my way out.
    Kari was looking at my pants. "Pull yourself together and don't forget to close your fly!"
    "Good idea!"
    "Bye, sweetie," she waved, as she took off.

I made my way to the intensive care unit. I had a splitting headache from the wine. Cutter had finished our morning surgical rounds and was sitting at the nursing station reviewing Mr. Peterson's chart.
    "Hey, man," I said, trying to be as casual as possible. Maybe he hadn't noticed I was late.
    "Where the fuck were you?"
    "At the lake."
    "You look like shit. Look at the way you're dressed. Have you lost your mind?"
    "Cutter, I had an unbelievable night."

"Unbelievable? You smell of liquor. Mick, you've gone crazy. You're going to be in big trouble. Harshberg will be here any minute now."

"I don't care. If you only knew how I felt last night."

"Get out of my face, you drunk bastard," Cutter said. "You're going to lose your job if you don't get the fuck out of here. Get your ass to the call room, take a shower, put on some clean scrubs, drink a jug of coffee and don't go anywhere unless I call you. Go now, or else you're going to get fucked big time."

The couch in the call room looked so inviting. I told myself I'd only lay down for five minutes. Half an hour later, I was awakened by the shrill beep of my pager.

"Good morning, Dr. Baldi," Ron, the scrub nurse, said on the telephone. "Drs. Harshberg and Ungaman are waiting for you in OR seven. It's the Duffy case."

"I'll be there in two minutes."

Frantically, I splashed my face with cold water slipped into a clean pair of surgical scrubs and flew to the operating room.

"Good morning, Rastus."

"Good morning, sir."

"I heard what happened to you, son," he continued.

I shot a cold stare to Cutter.

"Sorry to hear you're having belly pain," he added. "I know exactly how you feel. Couple of weeks ago, my kids gave me the stomach flu. I was barfing up intestinal contents and felt horrible. I hope you're feeling better after your nap this morning."

I looked back at Cutter and smiled. "I'm a bit better. Thank you for asking, sir."

"I appreciate you showing up to work today. Rastus, you're an important member of this team."

If he only knew the truth, I thought to myself. But he didn't and I was lucky that Cutter was my friend.

"Come stand next to me, Rastus," Harshberg said.

Cutter turned pale. "Sir," he immediately said, "I think we should let him cut open the chest this morning."

At first I didn't understand why Cutter recommended this. Then it dawned on me that he was trying to get me on the opposite side of the table and as far away from Harshberg as possible. He was afraid that Harshberg would smell the alcohol on my breath. Was he such a good friend that he would jeopardize the life of a patient by letting someone who was hungover operate? That seemed pretty unbelievable to me.

"Good idea. Rastus, go to the other side," Harshberg said.

I obeyed.

"Knife to Dr. Baldi," said Harshberg. He grabbed Mrs. Duffy's left chest with both hands and slightly lifted it off the table. "Go ahead, son. You know what to do."

I looked down at her skin and hesitated.

"Go ahead, son."

My right hand was shaking too much, undoubtedly from all the wine and coffee.

"Cutter, grab that knife from him. Rastus is incapable of cutting," Harshberg ordered, after I hesitated several times. "We can't expect him to do this. He's a radiologist!"

"Sir, it's his first time. He's never opened a chest before. Let's give him a chance."

"He'll cut all over the chest the way he's shaking."

I gave up. "Here," I said to Cutter, offering him the knife, but he declined.

"Rastus, are you giving up? Not on my service, son," Dr. Harshberg hurried to say. "You're going to do this. Cutter, come over here."

Cutter went to the opposite side of the table. "Sir?"

"Grab the chest for Rastus," he said, as he moved closer to the patient's feet. "Dr. Gastein, will you please unlock the table?"

"I already did."

"Rastus, hold that knife with both hands and apply it firmly to the skin," he instructed as he watched me do it. "Good. Now hold still, Rastus. Don't move." He grabbed the table and moved it back and forth to accomplish the skin incision. Everyone laughed as I stood there with the knife in my hands.

"If you can't bring the surgeon to the patient, you bring the patient to the surgeon," Cutter said. He was more than happy to have an occasion to use one of his jingles.

"It's amazing how much a brain-dead intern can do," Harshberg said, as he looked at me and smiled.

"Chest retractor to Dr. Ungaman," he ordered.

Cutter spread Mrs. Duffy's ribs with the large metallic retractor. "Let's see where her mass is."

"It should be in her upper lobe," added Harshberg.

"Here it is," I said as I pointed to an ugly looking tumor.

"Looks like cancer, boys. Don't you agree?"

Cutter felt it. "No doubt, sir."

"See, Rastus. Now you know why we always cut it out when we're in doubt. I feel better about our conversation with her last week."

"*When in doubt, we always cut it out,*" chanted Cutter.

"Rastus, switch places with Cutter," Harshberg said. "Clamp to Dr. Baldi and knife to Dr. Ungaman."

Inger delivered the instruments as requested. Cutter dissected out the mass as I held it for him with the clamp. Harshberg stood on the other side of the table with his hands rested on the chest retractor.

"It's a small tumor," said Inger, after taking a peek.

Harshberg nodded. "Boys, you just won't believe what happened to me last weekend," he said.

"Wild sex!" I replied without thinking.

"Wild sex? I don't even remember the last time I had any sex!" he joked. "The only excitement I get these days is from big toys. I just bought myself a brand new Ford Explorer after waiting two months for the dealer to deliver it."

"How does it drive?" Cutter asked.

"I couldn't really tell you because the minute I drove it off the dealer's lot I was in a major wreck."

"No shit?"

"This fuckin' idiot was driving an old Buick in front of me. The traffic was moving pretty good, then, out of nowhere, the guy stopped at a green traffic light to take a right. No warning, nothing. His rear lights weren't even working."

"So, you rear-ended him?" Inger asked.

"At sixty miles an hour. The Ford Explorer was so badly damaged that none of the doors would open. I was stuck behind that piece of trash, they call an airbag. I got my pocket knife out and shredded it to pieces."

"How did you get out of the car?" Gastein inquired.

"Through the sunroof."

"What about the fellow in the Buick," Cutter asked.

"His car was really trashed and there was blood on his windshield. I wondered if he was dead, because if he wasn't, I was ready to kill him after what he did to my cowboy hat!" he joked. "I swear to God I was ready to kill the irresponsible son of a bitch. I mean, you just don't brake in front of people like that."

"I would have killed him, too." Cutter kissed ass again.

"Did you kill him?" inquired Inger.
"No, he was a priest. A goddamn priest. I didn't kill him. I ended up stitching up his smashed forehead in the ambulance."
"Where's your Explorer now?"
"The junk yard!"
"Are you getting another one?" asked Gastein.
"I have to wait another two months to get it delivered again," he replied as he looked at Cutter handing the tumor to Inger. "Did you take it all?"
"Yes, sir."
"Any bleeding down there?"
"Dry field."
"Good work team. Close the chest together and take the rest of the day off. I have a meeting downtown this afternoon. I'll see you in the morning."
"Thank you, sir," said Cutter.
"By the way, Rastus, Merck just arrived on the ward this morning. See him before you leave. Keep him happy. Guys like him can be a nightmare sometimes."
"Yes, sir."

Cutter turned around and faced me. "Do you want to close the chest, you drunk bastard?"
"Cutter, I owe you a big one. You stuck your neck out for me this morning. I really appreciate it, man."
"What's going on?" Ron asked.
Cutter told them about my arrival to the intensive care unit and Gastein laughed.
"I can't believe that you pulled this one on Harshberg," Inger exclaimed.
"I'm surprised he didn't smell you," Cutter said, as he handed me the needle holder and the sutures. "I was scared he was going to find out."
I told Cutter I would do anything for him from now on because he had demonstrated, in a big way, that he was my true friend.
"How about you start by telling us the full story?"
"What story?" I said, playing dumb.
"The lake? Paradise?" he replied. "Unless the whole thing was hogshit?"
"Yes, tell us all the juicy details," Inger chimed in.
"Ron, how about some country music this morning?" I asked.

"No music until we hear the full story, doc," he answered.

"Start talking or else I'll tell Harshberg the truth tomorrow," Cutter threatened.

"I'm not the type who likes to kiss and tell, but under these circumstances I don't think that I have any other choice..."

"You don't," Gastein said.

"Listen at your own risk, folks. What you're about to hear may change your sex life forever..."

- Nineteen -

"Hello, Mr. Merck. How are you today?"
He was positioned flat on his back with his right leg hanging off the edge of the bed. "My leg is killing me. Hey man, can't you give me something for the pain? Can't you take care of my pain?"
"I'll do my best to help you," I responded sincerely.
He wept. "Can't you give me something for the pain? Do something, doc," he begged.
"Right away."
He was in worse shape than the last time I saw him. "Why are you still standing here? Get me something. Get me anything. Get rid of my pain."
"Let me talk to the nurse."
"I hate pain. Drugs, doc. I need drugs. Give me drugs. Numb me up. I can't take it anymore."
"What kind of drugs?"
"Any drug. Anything that will kill this pain. Hurry, doc."
I walked to the nursing desk and asked for some Demerol, a powerful analgesic. She rushed into the room with her big syringe, uncovered his buttocks, and pierced his right cheek. "Aaaah," he sighed a minute later. "I feel better already."
Since it takes the average patient a good half hour before getting any relief from the medication, I wondered whether his pain was psychological.
"How's your foot?" I asked, as I stepped forward towards it.
"Much worse."
"Here, let me take a quick look."
"Don't you dare touch it," he warned.
"Mr. Merck, I need to see if it's infected."
"I just changed the dressing an hour ago. Don't touch it, doc," he said.
"But it's very important that I see it."
"No," he replied, shaking his head like a little kid.
"I promise I'll be careful when I lift the dressing off," I said.
"Only if you give me more pain medication," he demanded.
"Now?"
"Yes, now."
"But you just got some."
"I want more."

"Are you still in pain?"
"No."
"So why should I give you more?"
"Because I want it."
He was bargaining for power.
"Mr. Merck, we just don't go around giving patients drugs just because they want them."
"No drug, no exam," he firmly replied, crossing his arms against his chest. "Harshberg saw me earlier and said I can get anything I want."
"I'm sure he meant anything you want within reason."
"If you don't mind now," he said ignoring my last comment, "I'm going to watch my favorite show."
Although I had only met him twice, I was starting to hate his guts because he was being totally disrespectful. "Please shut off the television," I said in a stern voice as I reached for his foot and grabbed it. "I need to see your foot whether you want to or not..."
"Stay away from me," he cried out, as he tossed the remote control on the floor. "What is this? A prison?"
"No, Mr. Merck, it's a hospital, and we're here to take care of you. So why don't you just relax and let me do my job."
He laid still and let me uncover his foot. "So how does it look to you, doc?"
His gangrene had progressed. "It's infected."
"Am I going to die?"
"I don't think so," I replied. "We'll start you on an antibiotic and cover your foot with a cream."
"Am I going to lose it?"
I hated to lie, so I evaded the question. "What did Dr. Harshberg tell you?"
"He promised to save it."
"If that's what he told you, then that's what will happen. He's the boss around here."
"And you?"
"What about me?"
"How many operations have you done?"
"I just started this year."
"So you don't know much about surgery?"
"I know enough to be here today and take care of you."
"Can I get another doctor? Someone with more experience?"
"No, sir. I'm it. I'll be the one who takes care of you."

"How about Harshberg?"

"Listen, Mr. Merck. It's my job to take care of you, whether you like it or not. The only time you'll see Dr. Harshberg again will be in the operating room, but even then you won't be able to talk to him. Now, you and I have to work together. We can make life difficult for each other or we can make it easy."

"What do you mean you can make it difficult? Do you mean you can hurt me?"

"I want to help you get better and get you back home as soon as I can," I said, trying to maintain my composure.

"Do you really care if I get better or not?"

"Yes, I do. So are you going to help me so that I can help you?"

He thought about it for a few seconds, then extended his right hand for a shake. "I think I'm getting to like you, Dr. Baldi. You're all right."

"Good. I have to go now. I'll see you tomorrow."

"Don't forget to tell nurse Jan to give me more of that pain stuff when I need it," he said in a last ditch effort to get more drugs.

I stood in the cafeteria and looked for a telephone to answer a page.

"Baldi, here."

"Hey, sweetie, are you all right?"

"Kari? Good to hear your voice."

"Did you survive your day?"

"Barely."

"Did they say anything to you this morning?"

I told her what happened with Cutter and the rest of the crew. To my great relief, she was okay with me having told them about last night.

"What are you doing next Saturday night?" she asked.

"Why?"

"I want to see you again."

"I can't wait that long. It's six days away," I whined.

"So you miss me already?" she asked.

"I do. Unfortunately, I'm working in the hospital on Saturday night."

"Maybe I'll bring you dinner and we can chat."

"Before Saturday?"

"I can't. My mother is in town this week."

"I see."

"Can I bring Mexican food?" she asked
"With two bottles of white Chardonnay!" I joked.

- Twenty -

"DOCTOR BALDI. DOCTOR MICK BALDI, STAT TO THE SURGICAL ICU. DOCTOR BALDI, STAT TO THE SURGICAL ICU."

"What's going on?" I asked the clerk at the desk as I ran into the intensive care unit.

"Over there, doc. Room 16, it's Peterson."

I rushed inside and found two frightened nurses. "What's happening?" I asked Melissa, the nurse in charge.

"His pressure dropped. He ate dinner an hour ago and started complaining of stomach pain shortly thereafter. I thought he had indigestion, but Maalox didn't help him. Then, five minutes ago, he began to sweat and he complained of chest pain."

"Mr. Peterson, are you still feeling chest pain?" I asked, as I moved toward the head of the bed.

He mumbled something incoherently.

"His pressure is bottoming," said Melissa, who was obviously alarmed.

I lowered the head of the bed and told her to give him more intravenous fluids.

"Let's get a chest X-ray and an EKG," I ordered. "Maybe he's having a heart attack." I was uncertain. "He's six days out of his second operation so maybe that's what it is."

I circled the bed a few times trying to figure out if there was something else going on. As soon as I laid my hand on his belly, he started moaning. "That's strange, he shouldn't be having that much pain," I told Melissa.

"Maybe he bled again," she said.

"Not likely. He's been off the blood thinner for several days now..."

"Harshberg started it again this morning," she interjected.

"What?"

"I though you knew," she replied.

I looked up at the monitor and his blood pressure was at an all time low. He could be completely brain dead in a few minutes. "Oh, fuck! That's the problem. Call CODE RED and page Harshberg STAT." I turned to the other nurse and said, "you, get me a knife, quickly."

Gastein was the first to respond to the code. "What's going on?" he asked.

"He's bleeding into his belly. We need to rush him to the operating room."

He went to the head of the bed and started giving him oxygen. "Did you call Harshberg?"

"Yeah," I said. My adrenaline was pumping. "WHERE IS THE KNIFE?" I shouted.

"What are you going to do?" asked Melissa, as she handed me the shiny scalpel.

"Mr. Peterson, forgive me if you feel any of this," I said, as I cut his belly open using his old wound.

He didn't flinch.

"Can you see his aorta?" Gastein asked.

There was blood everywhere.

"I can't see it but I think I feel it," I replied, as I palpated his kidneys, slid my hand to the center and grabbed the large artery. "Melissa, call for blood."

"Good idea," added Gastein, who was trying to give Peterson some oxygen, while at the same time squeezing the bag of intravenous fluids. "Also, please call the operating room to warn them we're coming."

Harshberg was panting when he showed up. "Rastus, what's this mess all about?"

"He's bleeding again, sir."

"Did you cut open his belly?"

"Two minutes ago, sir. His pressure had bottomed and he was unconscious."

Harshberg stepped to the head of the bed. "Is he still breathing?" he asked Gastein.

"Barely."

"We can still save him," said Harshberg, who seemed unruffled by the turn of events. "Rastus, his life is literally in your hand. Whatever you do, son, don't let go of his aorta," he ordered, as he unlocked the wheels of the bed and slowly pulled it towards the hallway. "Gastein, I sure do hope you've digested your doughnuts already because we're gonna have to rush this one in!"

We were in the operating room two minutes later. Inger and Ron were waiting for us with surgical caps and gloves.

"Come on, people, we need to move," Harshberg said, as he covered his cowboy hat with a surgical cap and covered his face with a mask. "Inger, make sure I have my regular aortic set on the table. Rastus, are you still squeezing?"

"Yes, sir."

"Ron, page Cutter. I need him here ASAP."

"I already called him," Inger said.

"Gastein, is he recording any blood pressure up there?"

"Maybe."

"That's good enough for me," Harshberg replied, as he grabbed the aortic clamp. "Now, Rastus, when I tell you to let go of his aorta, exchange places with me quickly. Are you ready, son?"

"Yes, sir."

"LET GO," he screamed, as he pushed me out of the way and shoved his hands inside Mr. Peterson's belly. "Any pressure now?" he turned around and asked Gastein.

"Fifty systolic after you clamped."

"Fifty is better than zero. We can still save the bastard."

At that point, Cutter walked into the room. "Who is on the table?" he asked.

"Peterson," replied Harshberg. "Put on some gloves and let's get to work. I sure hope that you didn't have any exotic plans for the night," Harshberg teased.

"Are you kidding? Even if I did, I'd cancel them. I live for moments like this one," Cutter replied, enthusiastically.

"That's a healthy attitude, son, especially if you wanna become a good heart surgeon, because your life will undoubtedly be filled with trouble and chaos."

"And lots of country music," Cutter added.

Harshberg looked around the room and said, "Gentlemen, let's play God for awhile."

- Twenty-one -

Ever since Mr. Merck landed on the ward with his painful foot, my headaches doubled. His addictive and manipulative personality drove his nurses insane and no matter what they did for him, he always complained, making everyone on the ward a victim of his hostile and grouchy attitude.

"How is Merck today?" Cutter asked.

"Pissing everyone off who is within a quarter mile radius of his room!"

"Is he that bad?"

"Would you like to take care of him for a few days?" I asked, sarcastically.

"I had my fair share of crazy patients during internship. Just bear with it, it'll be over sooner than you think."

"Easy for you to say, Cutter. You haven't seen him since he got here four days ago," I responded.

"The boss told me he had a reaction to Demerol. What happened?"

"The guy must be a drug addict or something. He was asking for it around the clock. I wanted my sleep so I told the nurse to go ahead and give it to him. Next thing I knew, he was getting more Demerol than all the other patients combined."

"Did you try to talk to him about it?"

"Try? The man doesn't listen to reason. I warned him about the side affects but he ignored my plea to change his pain control regimen. I even got one of the docs from the pain clinic to talk to him."

"What happened?"

"He manipulated the shit out of him. So we kept giving him more and more of it until he finally had a bad reaction. He got blisters over his entire body."

"No shit!"

"Even his testicles swelled up and blistered."

"Ouch!"

"Yeah, right. But he accused me of trying to kill him with the drug."

"The man must be insane."

"I got a dermatologist to see him. "

"How about a shrink?" he interjected.

"One shrink won't do. He needs a whole department of psychiatry to work with him!" I replied.
Cutter laughed. "How are you treating his pain now?"
"Morphine."
"One narcotic for another."
"He just wouldn't shut up about his pain. The morphine kept him happy for the last day. I have to listen to his rubbish everytime I go into his room. But you know, I'm starting to like him. There's something funny about him, about his misery."
"What's that?"
"I still haven't figured it out. I'll tell you when I do."
"How is his foot?"
"Worse. When are we cutting him?"
"Tomorrow," Cutter replied.
"Harshberg decided already?" I asked.
"I've never seen him agonize over a situation like this one. The cardiologist said that Merck's heart is fucked so we should try to do the operation under a regional anesthetic instead of a general one."
"And Harshberg is comfortable doing that?"
"He wants to keep him alive and save his leg. Personally, I think we should go ahead and chop it off. I don't know why Harshberg is being so cautious. It's just an amputation."
"That's easy to say when it's someone else's leg!" I said.
"I guess. But Harshberg is going out of his way to help him. I can't figure it out."
"Maybe he reminds him of a relative or someone he cares about it," I suggested.
"I don't know. In any case, he has made up his mind. "
"So what's in store for Merck? The Harshberg Smoker Special?"
"Yeah. He's going to bypass the blood flow to his foot."
"Does it usually work?"
"For a while until it fails."
"So why do it?"
"To get an extra procedure out of him. First we'll bypass the blockage then later we'll chop off the leg."
"And the advantage?"
"It's called creative surgery, bill for two procedures instead of one."
"You agree with that?"

He smiled. "No, but welcome to the world of medical economics, brother."

"Do you think Merck's going to tolerate all of this?"

"I don't know. What do you think?"

"What I think doesn't really matter. I'm just afraid he's going to end up a big train wreck in intensive care."

"His heart is definitely going to be a problem. Where is he right now?"

"Third floor. Do you wanna see him?"

Mr. Merck looked like an Egyptian mummy. He sat up in bed, covered with white gauze. His legs were spread apart as the nurse rubbed his groin and testicles with the skin cream.

"Good morning, Mr. Merck. Let me introduce to you the chief resident on the service, Dr. Ungaman. He's Dr. Harshberg's first assistant."

"How are you feeling, Mr. Merck?"

"Doc, I don't think it gets any better than this!" he said, as he winked to the nurse.

"Anything else we can do for you to make your stay more enjoyable?" Cutter asked.

"Yeah. You wouldn't happen to have a cigarette on you?"

"I hate to disappoint you, sir, but I don't smoke," Cutter replied, as he moved closer to his bed and uncovered his feet. "I came on behalf of Dr. Harshberg to tell you that we have scheduled your operation for tomorrow."

"That soon!"

"Your foot can't wait much longer. The sooner we do it the better off you'll be."

"What type of operation are you going to do?"

"AX FEM, FEM FEM, FEM POP," he replied emphasizing the POP.

"What's it called again?" a confused Merck asked.

"AX FEM, FEM FEM, FEM POP," he quickly repeated.

Merck grabbed his head between his hands and said, "Stop, my head is about to POP!"

"Don't worry, Mr. Merck. It sounds worse than it is," Cutter reassured him. "Let me explain to you what we'll do," he continued, as he took a pen out of his pocket and drew four imaginary Xs on Mr. Merck's body to illustrate the principle of the operation. "What we need to do is link the artery from under your left collar bone to the one in your left groin, then put another extension between your two groins, and finally a bypass graft from your right groin to below your right knee."

"I thought you said one operation."

"Right."

"What you just described sounds like three operations to me."

"Kind of, but we'll do it all in one session. So it's really one operation."

"Am I going to survive all the cutting?"

"Dr. Harshberg seems to think so."

- Twenty-two -

"Rastus, are you looking forward to this morning's case?"

"Very much, sir. I've never seen an AX FEM, FEM FEM, FEM POP before. I can't wait," I answered as I stood next to him at the scrub sink in front of OR seven.

Cutter couldn't wait either. He was covering Merck with a sterile drape. "He's excited like a kid in a candy store. He'll be a fine surgeon when he grows up," Harshberg said, referring to his protégé.

"What makes you believe that?"

"He's got the instinct for it. Besides, when a young man like him chooses to be in the operating room over being with his wife in bed, that's a healthy sign for a surgeon!"

"I see."

"Cutter reminds me of my younger years. His eagerness to cut, his temper, his attitude. I just hope that he doesn't lose those feelings because I sure haven't lost mine. I'm as excited to do this case as I was for my first one."

"Really?"

"Better believe it. This stuff is better than sex!"

"Nothing is better than sex," I replied.

"With sex it's always the same. You come, she comes, and with time it becomes more like a boring routine than a pleasurable adventure."

"And surgery?"

"Unpredictable. You never know how things will go. Hell, anything can happen and things can sometimes turn sour faster than you think."

"So you prefer this to sex?"

"Son, I live for days like this one. I feel accomplished when I play God with someone like Peterson or Merck," he replied as he turned off the water and drained the water off his elbows. "Look, who could have predicted that we would be able to save Peterson from death? He was half way in this grave when we sliced his belly. And Merck, boy is he in bad shape! His body is all screwed up. His blood vessels are clogged up and someone needs to re-establish his plumbing in one way or another. And that someone this morning is me."

"Is he going to make it?"

"Are you trying to offend me, son?" he replied. "Rastus, no one dies in my operating room. I just can't let it happen, simply because if it were to happen, it would give me a sense of failure. And a sense of failure is detrimental to my work as a surgeon. I'm in full control of my operating room and I make sure that every patient gets out alive. And I'm prepared to do it at any price."

I listened to him. "Yes, sir."

"Rest assured, Rastus, that this morning Merck will leave this operating room alive, but in what shape I can't tell you. I guarantee you one thing, he'll be your headache in intensive care tonight. So get ready, boy."

I thought about what he'd just said. "I suppose he's a dead duck then."

"The odds are against him. But there's still a very small chance that we'll get him through this."

"Sir, why bother then?"

"He needs the operation. Besides, you remember his visit to the clinic. He begged for the operation."

"But the impression I get from you is that he's going to die sooner or later. So why not let him go home with narcotics to help with his pain? At least he can die with dignity."

"If I let go of this man, he won't go home. He'll go out there and find a surgeon who's willing to do it. And when that happens, everyone will think I'm a wimp. Besides, son, it's a good case for Cutter. He needs to learn how to sew the grafts. I can't deprive him of the experience. So, come on, son, finish cleaning your hands and join us for the fun inside."

It was exactly seven-thirty in the morning when we all gathered around Merck's body like a bunch of monks ready to conduct a ritualistic ceremony.

"Come and stand to my right, Rastus. Cutter, have you done this operation before?" he asked, already knowing the answer.

"No, sir. But I've seen it many times."

"There's always a first time, son. Where's Ron?"

"Right behind you, Dr. Harshberg."

"How about some country music this morning?"

"Dr. Ungaman brought a special CD this morning," he replied as he went to the CD player. "It's from REM."

"That group of boys from Georgia?"

"I believe so."

"What the hell," replied Harshberg. "As long as they're southerners."

"Finally, something I can enjoy..." Gastein sighed in relief.

"Are you sure you wanna be here, Dr. Gastein?" Harshberg asked. "I just saw a big box of fatty doughnuts delivered to the recovery room."

"Do you want me to get you some?" the anesthesiologist retaliated.

"Just joking. No need to take it personally," he apologized. "Ready everyone?"

Cutter nodded his head. "I've been dreaming about this all night."

Harshberg laughed. "All right then. Get me the MARKER," he continued, with a Bostonian accent, mocking one of his former professors at Harvard. He grabbed the purple pen from Inger and drew multiple lines on Merck's body. "What do you think, Cutter? Are you happy with their locations?"

"Knife to me," Cutter said, joyfully as if he'd won the state lottery.

"Go ahead, son."

He took the scalpel and cut through the muscles below the left collar bone, within both groins, and below the right knee. Harshberg assisted him with the cutting as I stood there holding the retractors.

"I think that's it," commented Cutter, pointing to the wound he inflicted under the collar bone.

"How does it feel to you?" asked Harshberg in reference to the axillary artery traversing under the collar bone.

"Soft. Not much plaque. I think we can graft to it," he replied.

"Good. How about his groin vessels? Can you feel them?"

Cutter put his fingers into the groins and poked around a bit. "They're hard. Very hard."

"Just like I thought," he commented. "Get your fingers out of the way and let me feel those suckers. What a piece of shit we have to work with this morning," Harshberg told Cutter. "But I don't see any other option, and since we've gone that far, let's do the best we can with his hardened arteries," he turned around and faced Inger. "Trochar to Dr. Ungaman, please."

Inger handed Cutter the large instrument in the shape of an African spear. He strained as he shoved it into the left groin wound and tunneled it under the skin towards the collar bone. "Man, I'm meeting a lot of resistance," he said, sweating.

"Push harder," Harshberg replied. "He has the skin of an alligator."

"Here it is," Cutter said, as soon as he saw the sharp end arrive in the chest wound.

"Good work, Cutter. Now, tunnel the graft under the skin and let's start sewing."

"Rastus, how are you doing, son?" Harshberg asked.

"I'm still here," I replied.

"Six O prolene suture to Dr. Ungaman," he requested as he helped with retracting the wound.

Cutter sewed the end of the graft meticulously to the native blood vessel in the chest. "What do you think, sir?"

Harshberg was quite happy with the result. "Let's do the groin now." He looked at Cutter. "You're sweating, too. Dam'it, what's the room temperature?"

"Ninety-nine degrees," answered Gastein.

"Ninety-nine fuckin' degrees! Are we in the middle of the Arizona desert or what? Turn it down before we fry," ordered an upset Harshberg.

"I can't. His body temperature is too low. If I don't warm him up, his heart will start acting up."

"Can't you do something else?"

"I'm sorry but the nurse forgot to put the heating blanket on him. Nothing else can be done at this point."

"JESUS CHRIST, GASTEIN!" Harshberg yelled in distress. "Why didn't you think about it before we started the case?"

"The nurse forgot..."

"I FEEL LIKE I'M HAVING HOT FLASHES!" he exclaimed.

"Estrogen pills work very well for hot flashes," I joked.

"Rastus, this ain't funny, son," he said, facing Ron. "Dam'it, I can't operate in this condition. Ron, go get a fan."

"It's against OR policy to use a fan. It blows microbes into the wound."

"CHRIST!" he yelled again. "You should have thought about the heating blanket before the case," he told Gastein.

"He can't get any colder..."

"And I can't get any hotter," he interrupted him. "Rastus, come here and hold his blood vessel. Inger, get me another gown and a new pair of gloves." Much to the surprise of everyone in the room, Harshberg proceeded to rip apart his surgical gown, remove his boots and strip down to his underwear. He yelled and swore as he did it. He was wearing a pair of colorful pink, red hearts covered underwear, but no one dared to say anything.

"Hum..." Gastein cleared his throat.

Harshberg quickly washed his hands and walked back into the room and got gowned and gloved by Inger. He had a hairy back and a flat ass. He stepped toward the table and pushed me to his right side. "Fans are against operating room policy," he mocked Ron. "Operating half-naked is not!"

I couldn't help but laugh.

"RASTUS!"

"SIR?"

"What's so funny, son?"

I hesitated to answer.

"RASTUS!"

"Siiir," I stuttered. I was afraid he was going to kick me out. "Why..."

"Why what?"

"I was looking at your cowboy boots. Why rattlesnake skin?"

"Rastus, you're a pathological liar, son. What were you going to ask?"

I felt trapped. "Why pink?"

"Were you looking at my ass, son?" he asked, eyeing me. "Answer me, Rastus. Were you looking at my ass?"

"I couldn't help but notice..."

"Notice my ass," he interrupted me.

"No, sir. Not your ass, but the pink underwear. I never thought that..." I hesitated to continue.

"Speak up, Rastus."

"It never occurred to me that you were the type who would wear something like that. It doesn't fit your character."

Much to my surprise, he seemed a bit embarrassed. "My wife bought it for me for Valentine's day last year. It's her birthday today and she begged me to wear them for the occasion. She has something planned for this evening."

"I see."

"It seems silly but you wait 'til you get married. You'll end up doing things to please your wife that you haven't even dreamt of."

"Yes, sir."

"Yes, sir, what?"

"You have to do things to please your wife..." I answered.

"I hate to interrupt this lovely conversation but can we keep going? This man has been under the anesthetic too long," Gastein requested with a smile.

"Cutter, let's do the groin now."

We spent the next two hours working on Merck's blood vessels and grafts. While Cutter was busy sewing vessels, I was busy thinking about Harshberg's underwear.

"Not bad for a first time. Outstanding work, Cutter. Let Rastus close the skin."

"Yes, sir," Cutter replied.

"And, Rastus?" I heard him ask from behind.

"Sir?"

"Look at me, son."

I turned around.

"My Valentine's underwear is my personal business. Just don't make it the subject of your cocktail conversation with the nurses!"

- Twenty-three -

After four and a half hours in the operating room, Merck was gurneyed to the ICU in stable condition. Much to everyone's surprise, he didn't even require a blood transfusion. But despite these encouraging events, I was still very worried about him as I lay in bed. Strokes and heart attacks are common after big operations like his. And in my mind, if anyone was at risk for a life-threatening complication, it was my friend Mr. Merck.

I distracted myself by thinking about Kari. It was midnight and I laid in my hospital bed missing her. I hadn't seen her all week and I was desperately craving one of her hugs. I thought about her long, blonde hair gently sweeping my face at the lake. Before I knew it, I had slipped into dream land.

Several hours later, my pager went off. I reached for the telephone and knocked it off the table. I cursed for a few seconds, got up to turn the room lights on and dialed the number on my beeper. I was afraid it was going to be a call about Merck.

"Good morning, Dr. Baldi. This is your five o'clock wake-up call," the telephone operator said in a honeyed voice.

"It's morning already?"

"Rise and shine, doc," she said cheerfully.

"I'm dead tired," I moaned.

"I can only imagine the busy call schedule you carry. I hope your day goes well, Dr. Baldi."

"I hope yours does, too," I said.

After a brief stop in the hospital cafeteria, I headed to the intensive care unit to see how Merck survived his night.

"Good morning, Dr. Baldi," said Margaret, the nurse in charge of the night shift, as she came from behind and laid her hand on my right shoulder. I held up his chart to review it.

"How has he been?" I asked her.

"No trouble at all. He slept most of the night. Dr. Gastein took him off the respirator about half an hour ago."

"It's amazing how well he's done so far. I expected him to crash on us last night. How do his wounds look?"

"I only had to change his dressings twice. Not much bleeding there."
"And the pulse in his legs?"
"No change."
"God must really love this man," I said.
Merck was asleep went I entered his room.
"Good morning, Mr. Merck," I said, touching his leg. He didn't respond.
"Goooood mooooorning," I repeated.
His eyelids twitched but remained closed. A few seconds later, he uttered, "what's so good about it?"
"Isn't it a joy to be alive and well?"
"Speak for yourself," he said, opening his eyes.
"Life is good for you, too, my friend. You made it. How do you feel?"
"Like shit."
"Under the circumstances, that's understandable. Anything bothering you in particular?" I asked, while examining his wounds.
"Yeah, my back."
"What about it?"
"It's killing me. Can't you adjust it?"
"Adjust it?"
"Isn't that what a chiropractor is supposed to do?"
He was definitely disoriented.
"Do you know who you are?" I asked him.
"Yeah. Barry. Barry Cuda."
"Do you know where you are right now?"
"The Florida keys."
"And what year is it?"
"The year of the blind, Dr. Baldi," he said, laughing uncontrollably.
He'd been pulling my leg.
"So you remember my name?" I asked, just to be sure.
"And your face. I wouldn't forget your bald head in a million years..."
"I beg you not to bring up the issue of my baldness again..."
"Sorry, I forgot it's a sensitive thing for you."
After a couple of minutes of awkward silence, I said, "well, I'm glad we were able to save your leg and keep you alive."
"How about some breakfast this morning to celebrate?"
"Maybe lunch or dinner. I don't want you to get sick to your stomach with all the pain medications you've been receiving."

"Then how about a trip to the patio this morning to celebrate with one of these babes?" he asked, as he pulled a packet of Marlboro cigarettes from under his pillow.

"Where did you get those?" I demanded to know.

"I have connections," he grinned.

"You almost lost your life yesterday and here you are, asking for the same thing that got you sick in the first place. You're pathetic," I said. Any sympathy I had for the guy vanished in an instant.

"But I didn't die and now I want to celebrate," he pleaded.

"No cigarettes as long as I'm your doctor."

"Simple then."

"What's simple?"

"You're fired. I don't want you as my doctor effective now," he replied, in a stern voice.

"No, you've got that wrong, I'm firing you," I retaliated. "I'm sick and tired of your attitude."

"And of my bitching?"

"Yes."

"And the headaches I give you?"

"Yes."

"And my unreasonable complaints?"

"Those too."

Merck broke into tears. No one had ever talked to him like that. "You hate me," he said, in a broken voice.

"I didn't say I hated you."

"If you don't hate me, what do you feel towards me?" he asked.

"I'm just glad you're alive. Now, if you want me to be your doctor, you need to give me your cigarettes," I demanded.

"Only if you say that you don't hate me," he replied.

"I don't hate you, Mr. Merck."

That cheered him up a bit.

"I'm sorry for all the trouble..." he said, as he handed over the cigarettes. "You're the only friend I have, the only one who truly cares about me."

- Twenty-four -

The week flew by and before I knew it, Saturday was here and Kari and I were eating Mexican food in my hospital's room. Instead of white wine, she brought two bottles of French apple cider. Eating with her was a joy. I could definitely get used to having her around to take care of me.

"I like my coffee the way I like my men, strong and sweet," she said, as she poured sugar into her mug.
"Thank you for bringing dinner tonight," I replied, hugging her from behind.
"Feels great when you touch me, Mick."
I rubbed my lips up and down her neck. "You smell good, Kari," I whispered as I sniffed her beautiful hair.
"Did you miss me?"
"Like crazy. But things have been so hectic on the Harshberg service I hardly noticed the week go by."
"Anything interesting happen?" she inquired.
"Yeah, Peterson crashed again."
"No fuckin' way!"
"He bled like a stink after Harshberg restarted him on the heparin. Luckily, I was right around the corner from the intensive care unit when it happened, so I opened his belly and grabbed his aorta..."
"Wow, pretty aggressive!" she said.
"I didn't even think twice about it."
"Very gutsy."
"I know, but Harshberg had warned me that if I ever found myself in a situation like that I should act promptly to give the patient a chance."
"I wish I was there to see it," she replied excitedly.
"You would have loved it. It was chaos at its best with bright red blood squirting everywhere."
"Was anyone there to help you?"
"Gastein got there first and Harshberg stepped in shortly thereafter. I sat on Peterson's bed, holding his aorta, while the two of them rushed us to the operating room. Harshberg was yelling and cursing, and the whole thing felt like riding on a Western wagon with bunch of wild Indians chasing us!"
"Did he die?" she asked.

"We saved him. But the poor man had a stroke on the right side of his body and lost his kidneys in the process. If he survives his stay, he's going to need dialysis for the rest of his life."

"Oh, dear."

"Shit happens. We told him about all of the risks, when he first came to the clinic."

"Honestly, do you think he's going to survive all of this?"

"He's not out of the woods yet."

"It's sad, especially since he seemed like such a nice man when I first met him."

"I know. Luckily he has an understanding and supportive family. His wife hasn't left his bedside since his third operation."

"That's sweet."

"Yeah. Hey speaking of wild patients, I admitted this weirdo to our service on Monday. You'll meet him when you get back to work next week."

"What's his name?"

"Merck. He's quite an interesting character, hilarious, cynical, but at times the biggest pain in the ass!"

"I can't wait to meet him. By the way, Inger called me and told me what happened the other day."

"What?"

"Harshberg's Valentine underwear!"

"I'll never forget that scene," I replied as I got up and sat next to her on the hospital bed. "Speaking of scene, I loved the lake..."

"Me, too," she purred.

"I've been wondering though, what happened over there?"

"What do you mean what happened? You don't remember?"

"I remember when we started drinking and talking, but not the rest."

"What do you need to know?" she asked.

I cleared my throat. "Did we do it?"

"Too bad you forgot, doc," she teased.

"Did we?"

"Are you done eating?" she asked, as she began clearing the food from the table.

"Kari, please. What happened?" I begged.

"I'll never forget how beautiful it was..." She paused.

I raised my arms up in the air. "All right! We did it."

"No," she replied with a sad voice.

"What?"

"We talked a lot and by the time we got to it, you fell asleep under me and started snoring! I laid next to you and watched the stars until I fell asleep, too."

"Damn."

"It would have been nice, Mick. I really wanted to," she replied as she came back to the bed and started kissing my neck.

"Kari, maybe you should have tried to wake me up."

"I tried, Mick."

"Maybe you didn't try hard enough," I complained, as I grabbed her head with both of my hands and sucked her lips.

She pushed me back and smiled. "I tried hard, Mick, but it was you who couldn't get a hard on!" She giggled.

"Bullshit. I can deliver at any time."

"Oh, yeah..."

"Feel this," I whispered, as I led her hand down my belly until it landed in my groin.

"I'm really impressed, doc," she said, as she leaned backwards and removed my shoes.

"Wait."

"What?"

"Is the door locked?" I asked.

"Does it matter?"

"We're still in the hospital. I'd kiss my job good-bye if I'm caught."

"Mine, too," she replied, in a devilish tone, as she continued to undress me.

"How about your clothes?" I whispered.

"Be patient, doc," she answered, as she sat on my chest and rubbed my head.

I felt happy. "You're gorgeous," I said, as I ran my hand up and down her silky hair.

"You, too, sweetheart," she replied, sucking my neck like a vampire. Within a few seconds her lips were feeling my navel. "You're excited, aren't you?" she asked.

"I'd be seriously ill if I wasn't," I replied.

As soon as I tried to undress her, however, she told me to stop. "Not, yet," she warned.

"Come on, Kari. I'm suffering."

"Good," she said. She stood up and fixed her hair. "I'm leaving," she announced abruptly.

"What?"

"I'm going home, Mick."
"Did I do something wrong?" I asked.
"No."
"You can't do this to me," I cried out.
"Why not?"
"Because you just lit me up like a firecracker."
"Good then."
"Good fuckin' what?"
"Now you feel like I felt at the lake when you fell asleep on me," she said, in a vindictive tone that astonished me.
"But I was drunk."
"It doesn't matter."
"You got me drunk. Remember, you had all these hidden plans with the chilled Chardonnay..."
"Bye, Mick," she said, as she headed out the door.
"Fuckin' bitch. Cock tease," I mumbled to myself as I punched the wall with my fist.

- Twenty-five -

After Kari left my hospital room, it took me forever to fall asleep. When I finally did, my beeper went off.

"Sorry to wake you up, doctor. I have Kari from the ICU on the other line," the hospital operator said.

"Put her through," I mumbled, half asleep. It was exactly four hours since Kari had left me naked in my room.

"Hello, Mick."

"I thought you weren't working tonight."

"I'm not. I'm calling you from home."

I was still fuming from our earlier encounter. "You mean you didn't get to torture me enough? It's late and I need to sleep. So, good night..."

"Wait, don't hang up," she begged.

"What do you need?"

"I'm not feeling well. I ache all over. I need a doctor to come see me at home."

"A house call?" I asked. "Doctors don't do that anymore."

"They do for special patients. Do you know of a good doctor who can check on me tonight?" she said, with a sultry voice.

Suddenly, I understood her game. "I'm available but I can only offer you an operation." I decided to play along.

"You can cut me any way you want as long as you inspect every part of my body first," she whispered, in a soft voice.

"Are you bullshitting me again?"

"I'm serious, Mick. I need you in my bed right now or I'll die."

"Are you sure your name is Kari?"

"Yeah, why?"

"You sound very different from the cock tease who left me with blue balls four hours ago..."

"A woman's feelings can change faster than thunder," she said. "Try me now, Mick. I'll suck every inch of you."

"Hum..."

"You won't regret coming over, I promise," she continued.

"Really?"

"My underwear is on the kitchen table, my bra is on the floor, and my breasts are waiting for you. I'm all yours," she said.

"But I'm on hospital duty..."

"Your only duty is me tonight. Come, Mick, you won't regret it."

"Oh, fuck. I guess when duty calls, one must answer."

I covered my naked body with a white coat, slipped into my blue surgical clogs, grabbed my pager, rushed down to the parking lot, jumped into my car and raced to her house. I was there in five minutes flat. She had left the front door open.

"To your right, Sir Baldi," she said, as soon as she heard me enter.

I locked the door behind me and headed in the direction of her voice. She had lined up each side of the hallway with a row of red and white burning candles.

"Where are you?" I whispered.

"Follow the candles, Mick."

Her voice came from the end of the hallway.

I stopped in front of her children's room. They weren't there. Finally, I found myself standing in front of her bedroom.

Classical variations of Bach played in the background. "I feel like I'm in a Victoria's secret shop," I marveled.

Her king-size bed was surrounded by two circles of pink candles and a row of burning incense. She sat, cross-legged, with her back leaning against the wall. Her body was barely covered by a short silk robe.

"Are you just going to stand there?" she asked.

"This is like a fairy tale. God, you're so beautiful. Graceful. Incredible..."

She wrapped her arms around me and squeezed me hard. "Men tell women lots of nonsense when they want to get laid," she said.

"But, I really do mean it," I replied.

"Hush, Mick. Just hush," she replied, as she showered me with kisses.

We spent the night together. Before the break of dawn, I retrieved my pager from under her pillow, covered her naked, beautiful body with a quilt and rushed back to the hospital, where no one seemed to have noticed my absence.

- Twenty-six -

"Rastus, what's the matter? You're not your usual self this morning," asked Harshberg, as we stood in front of OR seven ready for the first case of the morning.
"I'm fine, sir."
"No, you're not. There's something bothering you," he insisted.
"Someone gave me shit today."
"What did you do wrong this time?" Cutter asked.
"Nothing really. I was just following orders."
"My orders?" Harshberg asked.
"Yes, sir."
"Who gave you shit?"
"Dr. Cherry, the nephrologist. He bitched at me for not calling him earlier on Mr. Peterson. He resents seeing patients just for dialysis because he wants to be involved in their entire care."
"Sounds reasonable."
"But, sir, I was following your orders which were to consult with other specialists only when we truly needed them."
"I supposed I did tell you that. What else did Dr. Cherry tell you?"
"He called me a dumb intern in front of five other doctors and nurses in the intensive care unit. I felt like an idiot standing there listening to him."
"I see. Did you insult him, son?"
"No, sir."
"Maybe you should have. Some people only respond to unkind words," he said. Harshberg ordered Cutter to page Dr. Cherry.
"Sir, maybe we should do it after the first case." Harshberg looked at him with a stern face. "Okay. Okay, I'll page him now," he said.
We waited for the nephrologist to answer.
"Dr. Cherry? Hold on, sir. Dr. Harshberg would like to speak to you," said Cutter, as he handed the receiver to the boss.
"Dr. Harshberg here. I just finished talking to my intern and apparently there was a misunderstanding this morning. I'm calling to clarify. . . I'm fully aware of that, Dr. Cherry.

Interns can do stupid things at times. Now, the real reason I called you was to tell you that Dr. Baldi didn't appreciate the way you lost your cool this morning . . . No, you listen to me, you piece of shit. When my intern calls you to tell you to do something, it's because I asked him to do so. So the last thing I want to hear is some goddamn specialist telling me how to run my service. When my intern calls you it's not a request, it's a fuckin' order. I hope you get this straight once and for all. Don't you ever humiliate my intern in public or I'll dialyze the shit out of your rotten brain. If you have something to say, at least have the balls to call me directly to discuss it. Is that understood? Is that understood you stupid fuck? Good. You have a great fuckin' day, asshole," he yelled, as he slammed the receiver against the wall. "Rastus come over here," he ordered.

I hesitated to step forward because I was afraid he was going to shower me with his anger. "Sir?"

"What service are you on, Rastus?"

"Cardiovascular surgery, sir."

"Otherwise known as what service?"

"The Harshberg service, sir."

He raised his head with pride. "And what do we do on the fuckin' Harshberg service?"

"We save lives, sir," I mumbled.

"I can't hear you. Louder, son."

"We save lives, sir," I repeated.

"Goddamn right we save lives, and don't you ever forget it. We, the cardiovascular surgeons, are at the top of the food chain. We're the lions of this fuckin' kingdom they call medicine and we take shit from no one. Is that understood?"

"Yes, sir."

Harshberg wrapped his left arm around my neck. "If Cherry or any other asshole in this place ever gives you trouble, you let me know right away."

"Yes, sir."

"You and Cutter are my boys. And I like to believe that I take good care of my boys. Is that understood?" he asked, looking at both of us.

"YES, SIR," we yelled together.

"You're untouchable," he continued, as he lifted his hat. "But don't forget now. I'm the only one who is allowed to give you shit!"

- Twenty-seven -

Punto Penesco, off the coast of Mexico, known as Rocky Point, was a memorable vacation that Kari and I would cherish forever.

"Awesome," she said, cuddling in my arms as we watched the magnificent sunset from the patio of a Mexican restaurant that overlooked the ocean.

"Think of all the days we miss out on beautiful things by working in the hospital," I said.

"The only thing I want to think about now is you," she said, lovingly.

"More drinks?" the Mexican waiter asked.

"Four margaritas with lots of salt," Kari hurried to reply.

"This stuff is the best I've ever tasted," I added, slurping up the last bit left in my glass.

"I can't believe you're halfway done with internship," Kari said.

"I know. Time melts away like a candle, leaving behind many memories. But we have so little time away from the hospital. I had to cover the services of four other interns for four weekends in a row to get these three days off to come here with you."

"Internship will be over sooner than you know. And you will be left with all the memories."

"Yeah, with many memories, some more painful than others," I continued. "Who could have predicted that a year ago Mr. Peterson was dancing the two-step with his wife and now he's glued to his wheelchair in a nursing home?"

"You never expect horrible things to happen to good people," Kari reflected.

"But they do. His body is paralyzed and his kidneys hooked to a dialysis machine," I said.

"Did he need to have his aneurysm fixed?"

"Medically speaking, yes. But I wonder sometimes if we did him any good by curing one disease and giving him another."

"Do you think he would have agreed to the surgery if we knew he was going to have a stroke?"

"I really don't know because I never asked him. But I did ask Mr. Evans, the farmer from Minnesota."

"What did he tell you?"

"He didn't regret his decision to have the surgery. For him, getting rid of his leg pain was worth taking the risk of having a stroke."

"But Mr. Peterson didn't have any pain," she pointed out.

"That's true. But his aneurysm was like a bomb ready to explode at any moment. We did what we thought was right for him..."

"What Harshberg thought was right for him," she interrupted me.

"Maybe."

"By the way, did you ever hear again from your friend, Mr. Satan?" she asked.

"Merck?"

"Where did he end up going after his third operation?"

"I shipped his ass to a skilled nursing facility."

"Four margaritas with extra salt," the waiter said, as he laid the drinks on the table in front of us.

"Thank you," Kari replied with a warm smile as she sat up in her chair and grabbed one of them. "Cheers, Mick."

"To you, babe."

"Skilled nursing facility? Is he going to stay there for good?"

I took another gulp. "God, no. The guy would drive them insane. He's almost fully recovered and he should go home soon. The only problem is that he fell in love with his physical therapist and he's been begging me to keep him there an extra month."

"Unbelievable! I remember how worried you were about him not making it after his first operation."

"I know. We opened the sucker twice and Dr. Melstein from plastics did the skin graft on his foot. He went through it all without a single complication."

"He must have good luck."

"You better believe it. I guess Fred was right when he told me that luck is all that matters."

"To good luck, Mick," she toasted.

"To the sexiest woman in Mexico tonight," I replied smiling. "Um, this shit is tasty."

"Why don't you ask the waiter for the recipe when he comes back?"

"Why?" I asked, caressing her hair.

"We'll steal some limes from my neighbor's tree and make margaritas when we get home," she said. Happiness was written all over her face.

"Just like when we stole his grapefruits under the rain and ran naked inside your house..."

She kissed my right cheek. "Squeezing their juice over our wet bodies was the most exciting sex I ever had."

"Listening to the thunderstorm was my favorite part," I added.

She kissed me again. "You pour joy into my heart, Mick. I'll always love you even after you leave."

"Who's talking of leaving?"

"Nothing lasts forever, Mick. June is just around the corner," she said, referring to the end of my internship.

"So?"

"When June comes, you'll pack your bags and move to California, leaving me behind."

"Who said that?"

"Come on, Mick. You know very well what I'm talking about."

"No, I really don't."

"You're single and free. I won't blame you for letting go of a mother with three kids. There's someone better waiting for you out there."

I held her in my arms. "What if that someone was you?"

"I wish. I really wish," she replied, as tears poured down her cheeks.

"Aren't we being too sentimental tonight?"

"Sorry," she sniffled. "I love you too much and I'm afraid of losing you."

"Your smile is worth a sky full of stars. Your pretty face is the one I want to wake up next to for the rest of my life."

"Really, Mick? You mean it?"

"Absolutely," I said, reassuring her with a kiss on her forehead.

She freed herself from my arms. "Let's celebrate, doc. Let's drink to love."

"And to Mexico..."

"What a memorable night," Kari said as she sat naked near the edge of the water. She invited me to sit next to her on the sand.

I looked at the reflection of the moon on the sea. "It's so pretty out here. I wish we could sit here..."

She reached for my hand and pulled me towards her. "Kiss me, you fool, and stop talking," she ordered.

"You're drunk, aren't you?" I asked.

"Happily drunk, happily in love." She gently directed my head towards her uncovered belly.

I licked it and sank further down until my legs were covered by the waves. Kari rubbed my bald head as she moaned and occasionally whispered words of love. A while later, she was screaming in joy.

"Are you allright?" I asked.

"Heavenly. Just heavenly."

"I wish you that feeling forever."

She sat up and hugged me. "You do it so well," she said. "Why do some men like oral sex so much?"

"Do you really wanna know?"

"Why?"

"Because they spend the first nine months of their life trying to get out of the womb of their mothers to reach a hopeful world. Unfortunately, when they get out they discover how miserable it is. Disappointed, they spend the rest of their lives trying to get back in."

"You're always so philosophical, Mick."

"And always so in love with you," I replied.

- Twenty-eight -

The ACLS was an institution of traditions and rituals handed down from one generation of physicians to another. And one such tradition was the weekly surgical morbidity and mortality conferences, otherwise known as M & M. Unlike chocolate M & M, surgical M & M had nothing sweet about them. Although the official goal of the conferences was to discuss critical patients for the sake of learning, in reality the conferences were an opportunity for the senior surgeons to display their arrogant egos, ridicule the young doctors in training and, most importantly, settle old scores amongst themselves.

M & M took place every Friday morning in the basement of the hospital, two rooms away from the morgue. During the conferences, the chief residents of each surgical service were responsible for summing up the activities of that service during the prior week. There were a total of twenty surgical services, each named after its senior surgeon. Second to the Harshberg service, the Schinstein service, otherwise known as the belly service, was the busiest.

If God's gift to cardiovascular surgery was Harshberg, then his gift to belly surgery was Schinstein. The latter was world renown for his skills and knowledge in modern laprascopic surgery, most of which he had invented or perfected. He was admired by everyone at the ACLS and also hated by many. His unpredictable personality was an eternal source of stress and anxiety for those who worked with him, and the simple mention of his name was enough to terrorize most of the other doctors, except for Harshberg.

The two were the most powerful surgeons at the ACLS, but they despised each other. I never quite understood whether their hate was based on jealousy or a difference in opinions. Dr. Schinstein was a big proponent of minimally invasive surgery, mostly laprascopy. Dr. Harshberg, on the other hand, believed in traditional surgery, guided by the knife. For him, laprascopic surgery, which he labeled as 'television surgery', was for the lesser surgeons, such as the obstetricians.

Cutter and I sat in the back of the conference room as the last surgical service was being presented by Dr. Wilkens, the chief resident on the Schinstein's service.

"The belly service is next," he said, as he stood in front of the room next to the black board. "We did thirty cases last week. There was one major and seven minor complications. The major complication was the unfortunate death of a fifty-two year old man who showed up in the emergency room five days ago with abdominal pain. I was summoned by the emergency room physician at ten o'clock in the evening and saw the patient fifteen minutes later. An incomplete history was obtained from his wife. Apparently, he had a history of diverticular disease. He was feverish and appeared in significant discomfort. His belly was most notable for diffuse pain and was rigid like a board. His worrisome presentation prompted me to call the radiologist to perform a CAT scan of the belly..."

"Not so fast, Dr. Wilkens," Harshberg interrupted, as he walked to the front of the room. "A man lost his life and there's something we can all learn here."

Schinstein sat tight in his chair, bracing himself for the war that was about to begin. "Please tell us again what you found on your physical exam," Harshberg asked politely.

"A fever of a hundred and six. His belly was diffusely painful and rigid like a board."

Harshberg interrupted him again.

"Let's see if I understood you well. You wasted your time talking to his wife, then you laid your hands on his painful and rigid belly. Did I hear you right?" he asked.

"Yes, sir, you did."

"About what time did you feel his rigid belly?"

"Roughly eleven-thirty, sir."

"Almost an hour and a half after you were called to see him, am I correct?"

"Yes, sir," Wilkens said, as his eyes nervously scanned the room for Schinstein.

"And what crossed your mind at eleven-thirty when you felt his painful belly, rigid like a board?" Harshberg pressed on.

"I thought that maybe his large intestine had ruptured."

"You thought of a ruptured intestine. What an awful and painful thought. A true surgical emergency, if I can think of one. Do you agree, Dr. Wilkens?"

"Absolutely, sir."

"Please continue your story," Harshberg said, as he started to circle the room looking down at the floor as he carefully listened.

"The CAT scan showed a perforated intestine with a large amount of free stool floating inside his belly. As soon as I learned the result, I called Dr. Schinstein at home..."

He was interrupted again. "A ruptured intestine, just like you thought. Good guess on your part, son," Harshberg said, congratulating him with a pat on the shoulder. "Now, what time was it when you finally called your senior surgeon?"

"About two o'clock in the morning. At two-thirty we opened his belly in the operating room."

"And what did you find?" he sounded intrigued.

"A big mess. His descending large colon was perforated and his entire belly was contaminated with feces. We had to cut out most of his intestine and give him a colostomy. Despite our greatest efforts, his condition began to deteriorate inside the operating room due to infection. We closed him up and rushed him to the intensive care unit, where, despite aggressive rescucitation, he died. We tried our best," Wilkens said, as he concluded his presentation and returned to his seat.

"I guess, your best wasn't good enough for this man," Harshberg said. "Stand up, Dr. Wilkens, because I'm not done discussing his case yet. It was an unfortunate case because it should have been handled differently. Cutter, what would you have done differently?"

"I would have sent him straight to the operating room. Time is of essence here because the shitlands never forgive an indecisive surgeon," he answered with a grin.

Wilkens jumped in to defend himself. "We needed to know for sure what was going on with him. We didn't want to be too aggressive with him. Aggressiveness can be dangerous."

"FUCK NO, SON! People don't die because of an aggressive surgeon, they die because of a thoughtless, incompetent one," Harshberg exclaimed. "Your patient's only chance for survival was to open his belly right then and there."

"It's totally unfair to speculate when you weren't there," Schinstein shot back. "We needed time to find out what was going on with him."

"Time to send a dying man to see a stupid radiologist in the middle of the fuckin' night, when what he really needed to see was the edge of a sharp, shiny knife. And what did the radiologist tell you that you didn't already know? That his belly was full of shit?"

"The perforation..." Schinstein tried to reply.

"Your patient was floating in enough shit he could have easily sunk the Titanic inside his belly. You should have smelled your hand after you examined him," he said with a cynical smile. "There's no doubt in my mind that you killed your patient by waiting."

Schinstein attempted to fight back. "You're going a bit too far, Harshberg."

"I'm not interested in your opinion," Harshberg interrupted. He turned around and looked at Wilkens with his sharp, steely eyes. "I don't know what they taught you in medical school but around here we never take the shitlands for granted."

Wilkens was flustered.

"Which medical school did you attend, son?" Harshberg asked him.

"Harvard Medical," he replied.

"I'll be damned. Another highly intelligent northeastern boy with less than an ounce's worth of common sense. If I were you, son, I would write to the Dean of HARVARD MEDICAL and ask him for a refund for all the tuition you paid. Because if you ask me, they didn't teach you shit. Sit down, son. Just sit down," he said, angrily.

It was ten minutes after the hour. M & M had come to an end.

"Boss, you really butchered Wilkens this morning. Don't you think you might have gone too far?" Cutter asked, as we walked down the hallway.

"What do you expect, Cutter? They killed a man," he replied.

"Well, sir, we've lost of a few ourselves," Cutter said, trying to add some perspective to the picture.

"Yes, we have. But the ones we lost weren't salvageable to start with. That wasn't the case here."

"I see."

"Besides, I hate this fuckin' Schinstein. I don't even know why everyone thinks so highly of him."

"It's the power of his laprascope, sir," Cutter said, in a provocative tone.

"Cutter, I told you never to mention that thing in front of me, or else you know where I'm gonna stick it..."

- Twenty-nine -

"Good morning, doctors," said Linda, one of the respiratory therapists.

"Sweet morning," replied Cutter, who returned her smile.

"I love the color of your stethoscope, doctor," she said as she slid her hand down the instrument wrapped around Cutter's neck.

"Do you really?" he asked, going along with the game.

"Yeah, I do," she replied, licking the side of her mouth with the tip of her tongue. "But it's a bit too short!"

"It may be short, Linda, but for you it's expandable!" Cutter said.

"Oh, really? How long does it get?"

"I've never measured it, but we can do it together if you like!"

"Maybe later, doc," she replied, as she walked away. "Maybe later," she teased him again.

"Damn! I really wanna fuck her bad," Cutter moaned.

"I'm sure she'd like that. Everyone knows how much she likes you."

"Really?" he asked me.

"And she isn't the only one. I know of five others who'd love to spend the night with you."

"No shit?"

"No shit. You're a good looking fellow, Cutter."

"Who else likes me?"

"I can't really tell you."

"Why?"

"Because you're happily married. Or at least that's what you tell me," I teased him.

"I am. But I'd like to know who else likes me."

"Why? Do you wanna fuck around?"

"I didn't say that. I just wanna know who likes me."

"I'm afraid it would torture you if I told you, especially since two of them are hot babes. I think you'd better stick to your wife." I was testing his feelings.

"I love my wife. I'm happily married..."

"Good," I said, as we started walking towards the wards.

"But I sure would love to grab that Linda from behind and show her what I can do to her," he added with the enthusiasm of a horny teenage boy.

"I'm not sure you can satisfy her," I challenged him.

"You just don't know me, Mick. When I fuck, I really fuck."

"Really? So why don't you ask her out?"

"Because I'm married," he replied, disappointed.

"It doesn't mean a thing. What are you going to do? Suffer in lust?"

"I don't know," he said. He was obviously confused.

"Listen, sooner or later, you're going to do it. Your sexual fantasies are never gonna go away."

"You think I should do it?"

"I think you're insane if you spend your life longing for other women without doing something about it."

"What are you trying to say?"

"If you have strong feelings for women like Linda, you should decide what you want to do with your marriage."

"You mean divorce my wife?"

"No. If you're happy with your marriage then stick with it and stop complaining to me about your sex life. But if you have doubts, go with the flow. If you see someone else, two things may happen. You may feel happier with them, in which case you should leave your wife. If it doesn't make you happier, at least you know it was just a fantasy and you move on with your married life."

"Or I could stay married and have secret affairs."

Before I could comment, Harshberg walked in. "Good morning, boys," he said.

"Good morning, sir," we replied.

"Do we have any consults this morning?"

"Yes, sir. We need to see Mrs. Smith. She's in the intensive care unit."

"What's her story?" he asked, as we walked down the hallway.

"She's bleeding from her gut..."

Harshberg suddenly halted us. "Rastus, did I say something funny?" he asked with a serious tone.

"No, sir."

"Then why were you laughing behind my back?"

"Well. Just before you came, we were talking about Linda and how she has a crush on Cutter."

"Sir, it's only talk," Cutter was quick to add.

"Is she cute?" he asked.

"Yes, sir, she is. Her eyes can tame a lion and excite a monk," I said. "You should have seen how Cutter behaved when he saw her earlier."

Harshberg turned to Cutter and asked, "son, do you wanna fuck Linda?"

Cutter didn't dare look him in the eyes. "Sir... I never said I wanted to..."

"But you never said you didn't want to?"

"She's dangerously attractive. Maybe I do."

"Be aware of women like her," Harshberg said. "They're bottom dwellers."

"Bottom dwellers?" I inquired.

"I never told you the story of the old man who went deep sea fishing?"

"No," we both replied.

"An old man went fishing one day. He sailed his boat for a while until he came across a school of fish. Although he couldn't make much of their shape, he was intrigued by their pretty, distant colors, so he rushed and threw his line hoping to hook one of them. It wasn't long before he felt a strong jerk in his fishing rod and started pulling his line as fast as he could. He was overwhelmed by joy and excitement for he had never caught a fish like it. Finally, he yanked it out of the water. The fish had pretty colors, just like he'd suspected, but much to his surprise she was a bottom dweller, one of them ugly creatures with big eyes and thick rugged skin. He was so frightened by the sight he swayed back and forth in his boat until he fell in the water. The fish dragged him all the way down to bottom and drowned him."

"Shit," Cutter said.

"You've got to be careful, son. Hospitals tend to be breeding grounds for bottom dwellers. If you get stuck with one of them, you're really screwed. It's one thing to fantasize about Linda, it's another to sleep with her."

"Well..."

"It's a tempting world out there. You've got to be careful."

"So who's this Smith?" Harshberg asked, as we headed for the ICU.

"Thirty-seven year old mother of three, perfectly well until about two months ago when she developed belly pain. Her local doc thought she had the stomach flu but her symptoms went on for a while, so he ordered an ultrasound which showed free fluid inside her belly but nothing else. Meanwhile, she continued to go down hill and about four weeks ago, she landed on the medicine service with kidney failure. Dr. Cherry biopsied her kidneys but the pathologist wasn't sure what it was. Shortly after the biopsy she started bleeding into her gut. Dr. Spiegl scoped her gut from above and below and found lots of stomach ulcers. Her colon, however, was clean."

"How long ago did she start bleeding?"

"Two weeks ago. Consultants from at least ten different specialties are involved in her care. They think she might have vasculitis but they can't agree on what type. The course of her illness has confused everyone."

"Why?"

"Well, she suffered a stroke on the right side of her brain soon after she had a heart attack. They think it's because the vasculitis has inflamed her blood vessels."

"Did they treat her?"

"She's been given a couple of cycles of immunosuppression with Cytoxan and Prednisone which hit her gut with a virus infection and severe bleeding."

"Is she getting transfused?"

"Several units of blood a day. They don't know what else to do for her, that's why they called us to see her."

"It doesn't sound good," Harshberg said.

"I forgot to tell you her lungs are filled with blood and pus. They don't know if she has aspirated the blood from her stomach or if she truly bled into her lungs."

"She's fucked. She's going to die," Harshberg said, straight out.

"Why, sir?" I asked.

"In my many years of practice, I've never seen a patient in her condition make it out of the hospital alive. They go through hell and then die."

"I see," I commented.

Harshberg led us into her room, where an elderly man and a teenage girl were standing at the bedside. "Good morning, I'm Dr. Harshberg," he said as he shook the man's hand. "These are my two assistants, Dr. Ungaman and Dr. Baldi."

Mrs. Smith smiled with her half-paralyzed face. She was hooked to the breathing machine.

"Nice to meet you, gentlemen. I'm her father and this is my granddaughter," the man said, as he wrapped his arm around the girl.

"I was asked by your doctors to come see you," Harshberg told Mrs. Smith. "It seems that no one knows for sure why you're bleeding. Are you aware of that?"

She nodded.

"You're in a difficult situation, Mrs. Smith," he continued, as he laid his left hand on her left leg. "I'm here to talk to you about an operation. We need to take a quick look inside your belly to see what's going on. We may have to take a small piece of your gut out to stop the bleeding and to possibly make a diagnosis. Would you be agreeable to such an operation?"

She looked at her daughter, who reached out to her and hugged her. She nodded affirmatively.

"Do you have any questions?"

She grabbed the clipboard and pen that were hanging off the side rail and slowly wrote a few words. She motioned me to read them.

She had written "I love your tie, doctor."

Her pretty eyes were starring at my Disney tie.

Harshberg seemed very touched. "You rest well now because you have a long day ahead of you tomorrow."

As we walked away, Harshberg was uncharacteristically emotional. "She's my wife's age," he said.

- Thirty -

Watching Mrs. Smith, a beautiful and previously healthy woman, deteriorate as fast as she did, made me want to spend every free moment I had with Kari. The effect of illness and death and all the suffering I witnessed while caring for the Harshberg's patients had finally gotten me. But fortunately, I had a night off and I'd planned to spend with Kari.

"Mummy, you're hurting my hair," said Sandra, Kari's daughter, as she combed her hair. Her youngest brother, Sam, hugged her.
"Stand still. I'm almost done."
"Are you going to read us a story before we go to sleep?" he asked.
She looked at me. "Uncle Mick will."
"Which one, uncle Mick?" he asked as he wrapped his small arms around my left leg.
"The Wild Swans," I replied, lifting him up and carrying him to his sister's bed.
Kari brought Sandra and sat her next to him on the bed. "Good night, sweethearts," she said. She kissed both of them and walked next door to check on their brother.
"Good night, mummy," they both replied.
"Where should I sit?" I asked them.
"Come between us," Sandra said.
"Boys and girls, are you ready for the story?" I asked.
"Yes, uncle Mick."
"Before we start, let me tell you a little bit about swans in general," I said, pointing to a picture of the bird. "The beautiful white animals swim in lakes and ponds. They're special because they live as couples..."
"What is a couple?" asked Sam.
"A boy and a girl, just like you and your sister," I replied.
"Like you and mummy, right?" added Sandra.
"Like me and mummy," I replied. "Swans are special because when two of them live together, if one dies, then the other lives alone forever."
"Is that what would happen to mummy if you die?" she asked me.

"We'll have to ask mummy tomorrow morning. Are you ready for the story?" I tried to evade her question.

"Yup."

I opened the fairy tales of Hans Christian Andersen and read to them for about twenty minutes until they fell asleep.

"How did it go?" asked Kari, as she exercised on the floor of her bedroom with her dumbbells.

"They're so bright."

"They love being around you."

"I love being around their mom," I replied, as I watched her do her evening routine of curl ups. "Especially when she models her strong, muscular body to me," I joked.

"Are you making fun of my muscles?"

"No, just of how compulsive you are when you exercise."

"Unlike you, doc, I need to take care of my body and stay in shape."

"Are you implying, I'm out of shape?" I asked her.

"I'm just saying your lazy," she replied with a smile. "Come on, get up and do a few with me."

"I don't need the exercise. Besides, I get tired just watching you do it."

"Look at your skinny arms," she added. "Aren't you ashamed at how weak you are?"

"Weak? I can wrestle you with one arm and win anytime of the day, even after a two-day shift at the hospital," I replied.

"I bet you a hundred dollars, you can't," she said. She dumped her weights on the floor and jumped on top of me.

I flipped her on the bed and sat on top of her, nailing both of her arms under my knees. "You can always try but you can't win," I said.

"You like to be on top. Don't you?"

"It's better than being on the bottom. Don't you think?"

"You look so cute when you're on top of me," she added affectionately. "Come and give me a kiss."

I leaned over to kiss her and she stuck her right knee in my groin and threw me forward. I hit my head against the wall. "OUCH!" I cried. "You hurt me."

She rubbed my scalp and hugged me. "I'm sorry."

"You tricked me. That wasn't fair."

"No one said life was fair," she replied, then kissed me and started undressing me.

After making love, we took a shower together. "I feel great," she said, as I scrubbed her body with olive oil soap.

"You make me happy," I told her, as we laid in bed, wrapped in warm towels.

"You, too," she said.

"I wish I could feel like this all the time."

"It would be nice. Wouldn't it?" she replied. "Good night, Mick."

"Good night, Kari," I said. I reached for the lamp and turned it off.

A few minutes later, I heard sniffles.

"Are you crying?" I asked. She remained quiet. "What's the matter?" I asked, as I rolled her body toward me.

"I have mixed feelings about all of this," she finally said.

"What did I do?"

"Nothing. I'm just afraid."

"Afraid of what?"

"I'm worried about the kids. They're getting too attached to you."

"So what's the problem?"

"You're leaving in four months."

"I thought we already talked about this..."

"I know."

"Kari, I'm leaving in June, but it doesn't mean that it's over."

"I'm afraid of getting hurt again."

"Why?"

"Because I've been hurt in the past..."

"It wasn't my fault if you were. Besides, I can't do much about your past."

"I know," she replied, drying her tears.

"What do you want me to do?"

"I don't expect you to do much. I care a lot about you. I'm always happy with you. But I can't take a chance with the kids."

"What do you mean?"

"I can't go on like this. The kids will end up getting hurt. If I were by myself I wouldn't care. But not with the kids. I'm setting them up for another emotional disappointment. They've been screwed up before and I can't let them go through it again."

"Kari, you know how much I love being a part of your family. But I can't commit to you this fast. We're still trying to get to know each other."

"I know. But I'm really afraid."

"You have to trust that I love you. Loving me back is a chance you have to take."

"I'm not sure I want to take that chance," she replied, coldly. "You only have to think about yourself. I have to think for all of us."

"I know. But you can't ask me to do something I'm not ready to do."

"I'm not asking you to marry me. Listen, all I want to do is to take care of my kids. They're the priority in my life right now. I guess what I'm trying to say is that I don't see any point in going any further. I'm really sorry."

I suddenly felt the urge to make love to her again. "Please," I begged, as I tried to kiss her again. "I'm dying to make love to you."

She was frigid. "I'm sorry, Mick, but making love won't change anything."

The pain of being around her was intolerable. I got up and put my clothes on.

"Where are you going?" she asked.

"I'm leaving," I replied, almost choking on my tears.

"You don't have to leave tonight. You're welcome to sleep next to me."

"It hurts too much being here with you," I said, as I opened the door and left.

She rushed after me naked. "Aren't you at least going to say good-bye?" she asked, as she stood on the sidewalk.

I hesitated, then hugged her. We cried together.

"Is this truly the end or am I dreaming?" I asked, as my hope for continuing this romance quickly faded before my very eyes.

"I'm afraid it's the end," she said, as she left my arms and slowly closed the door behind her.

I stood on the sidewalk wondering for twenty minutes whether I should follow her back inside the house.

- Thirty-one -

Life without Kari was unbearable at times. I missed her terribly but there was very little I could do to get her back. Occasionally I would bump into her in the ICU. Every time I did, I felt a deep ache inside my heart. Surprisingly, she seldom took care of patients on the Harshberg service after our break up. Planned or unplanned, I felt like she was avoiding me.

"Hey, Dr. Baldi. Is it true you ordered this olive oil for me?"
"I did, Mrs. Smith. Since you haven't been able to hold anything down in your stomach because of the ulcers and the infection, I thought olive oil may help you."
"I know it's good for the heart. But what can it do for me?"
"Olive oil will soothe your stomach and hopefully get rid of your nausea."
"Does it really work, doctor?" she asked with her caring, tired eyes.
"It has been used for ages in the Mediterranean countries. It helps heal ulcers and wounds because it has a fair amount of vitamin E mixed with some good fats. You should take some to lubricate your esophagus and stomach."
"Do I have to drink it?"
"Just take two tablespoons three times a day," I replied.
"Only if I see you do it first," she said smiling as she sat up in her ICU bed.
I turned around and faced Silvia. "Where's the magic oil?"
"Right here, Dr. Baldi. Food services brought her a cup from the cafeteria."
I poured myself a big tablespoon and swallowed it in front of Mrs. Smith and her husband. She grinned. "You really did it."
"I wouldn't order something for you that I wouldn't take myself. Come on, now. You have to try it."
"Okay," she replied. She sat up in her bed and bent forward with her mouth open. I sat next to her and grabbed her chin with my left hand as I slowly fed her the deep green olive oil.
"How was it?"
"Not as bad as I thought. Actually, I really like the taste."

"You're going to get better," her affectionate husband said, reassuringly.

"When you leave the hospital, I'll get you a jug full of it," I added.

"You really think I'm going to leave the hospital?" she asked with her tender voice.

"I hope so. You've been here two months already. Don't you think it's enough?" I replied.

"I know but I keep getting sicker and sicker all the time."

"You had two bad months but so far you beat the odds. I'm very optimistic."

"Honey, you heard the doctor. You're doing better already," her husband echoed, desperately.

"I really hope so," she replied. "Do you want to show Dr. Baldi the catalogue?"

"What catalogue?" I asked.

"Right here, doctor," said the husband as he opened his briefcase and pulled out a home improvement magazine. "I'd like to restore our kitchen before she comes back home. Let me show you which ones she likes the best," he said, as he sat next to her and flipped through the pages of the magazines showing the few designs she had picked. "What do you think?"

"They all look great. When are you starting?"

"Next week. And when she comes home, we're going to throw a big party and you're invited."

"Thank you. I'll look forward to that day," I said. "I have to go. I'll see you again this evening."

"Doctor, can I talk to you for a minute?" her husband requested.

"Sure."

"Sweetheart, I'll be right back. I'm going to talk to the doctor regarding insurance paper work."

We walked out of the room and sat at the nursing station, just a few rooms away.

"Doctor, do you think she'll make it?"

"I hope so."

"Please, tell me the truth," he begged.

"Why would I lie to you?"

"I trust you. But I heard one nurse tell another that all the consultants seeing my wife think that she has no chance."

"That's not true, Mr. Smith. If the consultants truly feel that way, they would have stopped giving her the best care that they can. She's very sick and there's no way to predict how she'll do. But I'm optimistic she's going to make it."

"Why?"

"Because every time I look into her eyes, I see someone who wants to live. And as long as I see that desire, I'll do my best to help her make it."

"Do you think I'm too optimistic by restoring the kitchen?"

"I don't think so."

"You know what's funny, doctor?"

"What?"

"By the time we're done with all of this, we may not have a home. Her medical bills have already exceeded what her insurance covers. We've already lost half of our family business."

"I'm sorry to hear that."

"But that doesn't bother me, as long as she comes home again. It's all I ask from God."

"Your wife is blessed for having you next to her. I'm sure she's very appreciative of all your caring and love."

He was teary-eyed.

"You know, Mr. Smith, you've been through a lot already. Believe me, many husbands would have walked away. You've seen too much already."

He sniffled. "Why did it happen to her? She's never been sick in her life."

"I don't know why it happened to her. What I know is that we're all trying our best to get her out of this mess. She's trying hard, too. All the blood she lost, the three operations she had, all the endoscopies, all the transfusions, the many times we had to put her on the breathing machine. I've never seen a patient in my life on twenty two medications. It's a lot. Let's pray that she'll get better."

"I can't imagine living without her. She's young. I want her to live."

"I hope she will."

"I'm willing to take her back home in any shape she's in. If she lives I promise to take care of her for the rest of my life."

"I really wished that all the patients who come here had family members who cared as much as you do. She's been stable for the last three days. I'm hoping to get her out of the ICU by the end of the week. She'll be better off on the regular ward. There isn't as much noise there. She'll feel better."

"You really think she'll leave the ICU?"

"Let's cross our fingers and hope."
"That's great news, doctor. That's great news," he said, drying his tears with a bit of hope.

- Thirty-two -

No matter how hard we tried to beat up on Merck's weak body, the man was invincible. After four major operations, six trips to the intensive care units, and endless days in the hospital and rehabilitation unit, he was still around to harass the surgical staff of the ACLS. Despite Harshberg's miraculous surgical skills, his first three operations had failed and Mr. Merck's had to undergo a fourth complicated operation in order to save his beloved, gangrenous foot.

"Mr. Merck, what do you think you're doing?" I asked, as he sat on his bed with a Marlboro packet in his right hand.
"I'm gonna smoke one of them babies," he replied pointing to the cigarettes.
"No, you're not. You know that you're not allowed to smoke," I replied firmly.
"Listen to me, son. Don't start preaching to me again because I'm not going to listen this time. I've had it."
"You know that cigarettes are bad for you..."
"I know what I know. I've been told by every doctor and nurse not to smoke. But listen to me, young man, you try to stop me for puffing this one and you're in big trouble," he warned me as I tried to take away his cigarettes. "Get away from me, doc," he begged as he pushed me away with his left elbow.
"Please, be reasonable now," I said giving up.
"I've been smoking since I was thirteen years old. That's over fifty years. Now, I don't drink, I don't do drugs, I don't run around chasing women like I used to, and I can no longer have sex. I've been operated on four times so far this year. My leg hurts and I'm going to lose it soon," he said. "I've nothing left in this world, no pleasure except for these cigarettes."
"Maybe you lost everything because of your cigarettes."
"I don't care," he replied shrugging his shoulders.
"I do. You keep coming back for more operations. Your graft clogged up again and we had to fix it yesterday."
"I don't give a damn about my graft."
"Don't you have anything else to live for?"
"No."

"Oh, come on. Can't you think of something beautiful in life?"

"It's easy for you to say. But when you're my age and in my shoes, your options are limited. I'm fucked, so why don't you let me be, son," he begged me.

"What does your wife think about all of this, Mr. Merck?"

"Joseph. You can call me Joseph, doc."

"Joseph, what does your wife think about all of this?"

"Which wife?"

"How many do you have?"

"I have been married three times."

"Really?"

"You may think I'm an ugly old fart, but believe me, I had my days of glory when I was younger." He lit a cigarette completely ignoring my authority.

Afraid of setting off the fire alarm, I frantically closed the door and opened the window. "I never said you were. What happened to your wives?"

"You don't want to hear the story of an old man," he replied looking at the window.

"Yes, I do," I said, as I approached his bed. "May I sit on your bed?"

"Of course," he replied, moving to the side. "My first wife left me after seven years of marriage. I came home one day only to find out she ran away with my next door neighbor."

"Why?"

"He had money, lots of it. I was an average Joe with enough money to put food on the table and take care of the family's basic needs."

"Did you love her?"

"Yeah, but I never forgave the bitch for what she did to me and the children."

"Sorry to hear that."

"Money keeps the world spinning," he said, as he sucked on his cigarette.

"How about your second wife?"

"It was a mistake," he replied with a smile.

"A mistake?"

"I was miserable after my first wife left me. I met this girl in a bar one night. In the beginning, I didn't think much of her. But the more I drank the more beautiful she became. By the end of the evening, we ended up in her apartment doing the

Tango until I passed out on her floor. When I woke up I realized the big mistake I had just made."
"What?"
"I'd asked her to marry me."
"How interesting!"
"That Tango dance got me in trouble. I was stuck with her for nine months. Every night before we went to bed and every morning after we got up, I told her what a bitch it was to be living with her. Twice a day, for nine months. Finally she got the message and left."
"Any luck with the third one?"
"My third wife, I married because of love. We had twenty five years together. It was nice while it lasted."
"What happened?"
"I could no longer do it."
"Do what?"
"The wild thing."
"Sex?"
"Yeah, sex. One day I woke up and looked at my penis. Joseph junior went dead on me. I tried to reason with him, but without much response on his part. I shook him, I even beat him. Finally, I saw a dozen doctors who all told me I had a circulation problem because of my clogged arteries."
"I see."
"They also told me it would be a miracle if I ever had another erection. They were right. Joseph junior never pointed upwards since."
"What happened to your wife?"
"She ran away with a younger guy she met at the mall. Sex was important to her. She wanted it bad and I couldn't deliver."
"But I thought you have a penile prosthesis?"
"I do. But I got it after my third wife left me."
"Why? Did you have another girlfriend after her?"
"No."
"So why did you get it?"
"One of my neighbors got one, so I figured what the heck, I should get one too."
"But did you need it?"
"Never used it," he replied, lighting another cigarette.
"Strange."
"Strange, it is. But it's a penis-focused society, son," he responded, lifting both of his eyebrows.

"So, have you had any luck with the ladies since?"

"Luck? Son, if it wasn't for bad luck, I wouldn't have had any luck at all."

"Were you upset that your third wife left?"

"Not really, I felt more betrayed by Joseph junior. How could he turn his back on me?"

"Did you try to stop her from leaving?"

"Stop her? You must be joking, son. Do you know much about women?"

"A little bit."

"Listen, doc, when a woman has made up her mind, it's final. If she wants to go, she'll go. There's no point in trying to stop her. The more you try, the more you suffer. Misery is what life is all about sometimes. Enjoy the good days while they last."

"You've gone through so much. You must hate women by now."

"You can't hate them. They always do what's best for them. You just got to find the right one to live with, one who wants the same things out of life as you."

"Do you ever get lonely?"

"Yeah, a lot. Life sucks when you're alone, and tragic when you go through it by yourself."

"I know what you're saying," I responded thinking about Kari.

"How old are you?"

"Twenty-eight."

"Are you married?"

"No. I don't think I'll ever be."

"Don't say that," he responded, as he took a few more puffs and exhaled while looking out of the window.

"I'll never find the right woman."

"No, son, you will. And believe me, when you do, she'll knock your ass over a tea kettle. There's a woman out there for you, doc."

"You think so?"

"I know so."

"The right woman?"

"Yes, the right one."

"You tell me who she is and I'll call her tonight," I joked.

"Don't worry, you'll find her."

"Where?"

"Go to church, son. There are plenty of them there."

"What if I were Muslim or Jewish?"
"Go to church regardless. Love has no religion."
"So how come you don't go to church and find one for yourself?"
"I had my days, son. Believe me," he replied with a wicked smile. "I had my days."

- Thirty-three -

"Hello, Dr. Baldi. Mr. Merck is trying to reach you from his nursing home," said the hospital operator.

"Put him through," I replied wondering about what kind of trouble he was in. His problems were endless.

"Dr. Baldi, I hope I'm not interrupting something important," he said with his usual, hoarse voice.

"Not at all. I'm glad you called," I replied. "How can I help you?"

"I know I've been a pain in the ass all this time, but this time I'm calling you with some good news."

"What's going on?"

"I found you a lady," he answered enthusiastically.

"Really?"

"My nurse. She's wonderful."

"Um..."

"She's really cute, doc. You'll love her."

"What color hair does she have?" I inquired.

"She's not blonde, but she's quite something. You'll die when you meet her."

"She's that hot?"

"I'm in love with her, doc," he added. "But I figured I'm too old for her, so I want you to have her."

"It's awfully nice of you, Mr. Merck."

"Sweet, beautiful, nice breasts, and an ass to die for..."

"Mr. Merck!"

"Sorry, I get carried away sometimes."

"Does she know that you are trying to set us up?"

"Yeah, I told her everything about you and she's looking forward to meeting you tomorrow. I hope you can make it."

"Tomorrow?"

"I hope you don't mind but I promised that you'll meet her for dinner at seven. I know I got carried away. But I got excited for you."

"I don't know what to say..."

"Say yes. Say you'll take her out to some fancy restaurant. I suggest that expensive Italian restaurant downtown. You won't regret it, doc. She's worth every penny."

"But I don't know if they can fit us in for dinner on such a short notice."

BEYOND THE MAGIC SCALPEL • 133

"Don't worry, I already made the reservations. She'll meet you there."
"How am I going to find her?"
"She'll find you."
"What's her name?"
"Shelly. Be there, doc. You won't regret it," he said, before hanging up.

I never thought that Merck would reward my medical care by setting me up on a blind date with a beautiful woman. What if Shelly was the right woman I've been looking for all this time? What if our dinner date was the beginning of romance, love, and possibly marriage?

Excited, I got to the restaurant ahead of time. As instructed, I waited for her outside with a red rose in my hand. I found myself a wooden bench and listened to the opera music coming from inside the restaurant. It was April and the sun was setting at that hour. Everytime a beautiful woman came my way, I hoped she wasn't the one, because I was expecting a princess of beauty. Not that the women I saw were ugly, I was just hoping for someone better.

"Dr. Baldi?" she asked.
"Shelly?" I nearly fainted.
"Nice to meet you," she said, as she shook my hand.
"The pleasure is truly mine."
"Are you all right, doctor?" she asked, after she noticed my face.
"Yeah. I'm fine," I said.
Either she was the wrong person or Merck had set me up with the ugliest woman in town!
"Shall we?" she asked pointing to the door.
"Of course," I replied, trying my best to hide my disgust.
"We have a reservation under Dr. Baldi," she told the restaurant hostess.
"Oh, yes. Mr. Merck made the reservations for you. This way, please," she said, as she led us to a secluded corner. "This is your table," the waitress pointed. There was a bottle of champagne chilled on ice. "Mr. Merck ordered it for you. Enjoy," she said, as she laid the menu on the table.
"How lovely!" Shelly said, as she looked around.
"Indeed," I managed to say.

"So, tell me a bit more about you, doctor?" she said, as she ran her hands through her thick, black, curly, disgusting hair.

I sat with Shelly for a full two hours thinking of ways to end the dinner prematurely. I listened to her boring stories as she occasionally played with her facial hair. I'd lost my appetite early on, but she went through a six course Italian meal that cost me one hundred and fifty dollars. The entire time I was with her, I thought about one thing and one thing only: how to lay my hands on Merck's neck and choke him to death!

- Thirty-four -

"It's Saturday, boys, and I have a soccer game this afternoon. Let's fly through rounds and get the hell out of here," Harshberg said, as we stood at the entrance of the intensive care unit.

"Sounds like a good plan," Cutter replied.

"What's going on with Smith?" Harshberg asked.

"Her bleeding hasn't stopped. During the course of the last twenty-four hours, she was given fifteen units of blood."

"Shit," Harshberg said. "This lady is cursed."

"The gastroenterologist scoped her for the eighth time and tried to seal some of the bleeders in her stomach."

"Obviously it didn't work," he added. "How often is she getting dialyzed?"

"Every other day."

"And her lungs?"

"Still infected and filled with blood. She's not doing well on the breathing machine."

"What else?"

"Her liver is out."

"I guess it's the end of the road for her," Harshberg sighed.

"I agree," Cutter said. "But no one wants to make the decision to withdraw her life support."

We stood in front of her room. Her entire family was gathered around her bed. They were expecting us.

"Good morning, everybody," Harshberg said, as he walked to the other side of her bed and stood next to the respirator. He quickly glanced at the numbers on the heart monitor and shook his head. "It doesn't look good," he told them.

Her teenage daughter started crying. "Can't you do something for mom?"

"She just can't go on like this any longer. Her illness is beyond all of us and we need to let her go."

"Let her go? You can't let mom die," her son sobbed.

"I'm afraid there's nothing else I can do for her at this stage. She's dying in front of your eyes. Actually, as far as I'm concerned, she's already dead."

Her husband was ready to hit him. "We can't turn our backs on her and walk away. Do something," he pleaded desperately.

"Please try to understand. She has no chance," Harshberg said, this time trying to sound a bit more sympathetic.

"You can't just let her bleed to death," her uncle said.

"And we can't just keep transfusing her around the clock. She drained the blood bank supplies for the last two weeks," Harshberg said.

Her teary father stepped forward. "Please, Dr. Harshberg, stop her bleeding. We can't abandon her at this point. She can still comprehend everything going on with her."

"I've taken her to the operating room five times already. How much more torture do you want me to put her through? Why can't you just accept it?"

"Accept what?" her husband replied, crying. "That I'm losing the woman I've loved all my life."

His children hugged him. "Please, Dr. Harshberg, give her another chance," they begged.

"I'm awfully sorry. But she's dead and there's nothing else I'm going to do," he replied. "If you'll excuse us now, we have other patients to see."

"Bastard," her uncle shouted.

Harshberg rushed down the hallway without looking back. Instead of stopping at the ward, he kept walking until we reached the cafeteria. "Mick, you know her family better than I do. Please, go back and talk to them," he requested, a bit shaken. "They think I'm an asshole and I don't blame them. I understand their pain but there's nothing else I can offer her. You saw the mess inside her belly. Do you think we can salvage her?" he asked me.

"No, sir."

"It would take a miracle at this point to save her life and even if it did happen she'd be crippled for the rest of her life. I can't torture her anymore. Give them a day or two to absorb the situation, then take her off the respirator as soon as you can."

- Thirty-five -

"Dr. Baldi, here. I'm returning page."
It was shortly after midnight.
"I'm sorry to wake you up," Harshberg said.
"Actually, I'm not in bed yet. I've been taking care of Mr. Gray."
"What's wrong with him?"
"He had a heart attack."
"Anyone there with you?" he asked.
"The cardiologist, sir."
"Let him take care of it and come meet me in the ICU."

By the time I arrived in the ICU, Harshberg was sitting at the nursing desk in front of Mrs. Smith's room. For the first time since I'd met him he didn't have his cowboy hat or boots on. Instead, he was dressed in surgical scrubs and a pair of Nike running shoes.

He got up as soon as he saw me. "Let's go," he said, as he called for Silvia. He walked into Smith's room, unlocked the brakes of her bed and wheeled her to the operating room. She was unconscious.

As soon as Harshberg opened her belly, blood came pouring out. I suctioned it as fast as I could and helped him retract the muscles. He extended the incision from her breastbone down to her pubic area.

Her condition had worsened. Several pockets of clotted blood covered her liver and stomach.

Harshberg laid her intestines in his hands and felt them for a while. He gently reached for the antibiotics bottle and poured the solution inside her belly. "The only way to stop the bleeding is to take out her entire gut," he frowned. He thought for a few minutes before deciding to cut out her entire stomach and half of her small intestine.

After two hours of silence inside the operating room, he withdrew to a corner chair and patiently watched me close the belly. Once finished, we transferred Mrs. Smith to her ICU bed and wheeled her back to her room.

"Son, come meet me in the doctors' lounge in ten minutes," he said before he left the ICU.

I found him sitting in the lounge, starring at the television set. I poured a cup of coffee and approached him. He didn't say a word. He was obviously lost in his own thoughts.

"Sir, I thought you said she was going to die, with or without the operation," I said, finally breaking the silence. "Why did you take her back tonight?"

He turned around and smiled sadly. "You're young, son, too young. The more you see of this world, the more you realize it doesn't make much sense. You can think about it with your head for as long as you want, but sometimes you've got to go with your gut feelings. It may not make much scientific or medical sense, but you've just got to say, WHAT THE FUCK! I'll give it one more try." He reached for a bottle of Scotch whiskey hidden between his legs and took a generous sip. "Thirty-seven years old with three teenage kids," he continued as he looked out of the window. "Three months in intensive care with at least three hundred thousand dollars worth of blood transfusions. And in the end what did her family get? Nothing," he said, as he drank more whiskey. "Not only did her husband lose her, but he also lost his home and his business. This is heavy, son, very heavy."

"It was a tough situation, sir," I replied, trying to ease his emotional pain. "I'm sure her family appreciated everything you did for her. There's only so much you can do for people."

"Apparently, I haven't done enough for her. She's dying."

"You gave her your best shot, sir. You even gave her the extra chance her family asked for this morning..."

"I didn't do it for the family," he conceded. "I did it for my miserable soul. I did it so that next time I sit with my family, I'll have enough courage to look at my wife," he said, wiping his mouth with the back of his hand. "Willie Harshberg, chief of cardiovascular surgery, at the American College of Legendary Surgeons... Well, big fuckin' deal! When I was at the General in Boston, my mentor told me I was the best they'd ever trained. I wished the bastard was here tonight to see what kind of a shape this lady was in, because he would have changed his mind about me."

"Sir, it's not fair the way you're taking it on yourself..."

"Not fair? Go tell that to her husband, not me," he interrupted me. "I just can't believe this shit. Of all the thousands of operations I've done, of all the thousands of lives I've saved, of all the demented old farts I've revived to send back to some nursing home, she was the life I needed to save the most and I failed. Life just doesn't make sense, son."

"You did your best, sir."

"I guess my best wasn't good enough," he replied, teary-eyed. "Damn Harshberg."

His emotional breakdown made me feel uncomfortable. I tried to change the subject. "Sir, how did your soccer game go today?"

"Soccer game? I felt a knot in my stomach after Smith's uncle called me a bastard. It really affected me. I sat in my backyard all afternoon and thought about her. She's my wife's age and her kids just like mine. I thought about her poor husband. I felt sorry for the man. It was as if he was watching his wife drown in a sea. His head tells him not to jump in, because if he does, he dies with her. His heart tells him to jump in, because if he doesn't, the pain of watching her die kills him. Either way you look at it, he's fucked. That's how I felt all day, until I finally decided to jump into water. Not that it was going to make any difference, it's just something I can live with."

"Sir, you tried your best."

"Yes, I tried. Yes, I failed miserably."

He got up and headed towards the door, leaving behind the empty bottle of whiskey. He stopped at the door, turned around and looked at me.

"Son..."

"Sir?"

"Do this lady a favor and take her off the respirator tomorrow morning," he requested with a sad voice. "I'm not God and I just hope her family can understand."

- Thirty-six -

Mr. Smith couldn't watch his wife die. Instead he sat in the garden outside her window as thirteen family members surrounded her bed to bid her good-bye.

I flooded her body with morphine just before I turned off the respirator and pulled out the tube from her mouth. She seemed very comfortable as she slipped from the known to the unknown.

"Is she dead, doctor?" her daughter asked, after a long silence.

I stood near Mrs. Smith' bed and looked at her angelic face. Despite all her misery, she was still blooming with beauty. As I brought my face near her nose, to check for any signs of breathing, my own tears washed her face. I tried to gather myself and say something meaningful. "A philosopher from ancient Greece once said on his death bed, 'And now my friends it's time for us to depart each other. I, to die, and you to live. Whoever has the better destiny is unknown to all except to God'. I sure hope she's seeing her better destiny, now."

"Can you please close her eyes, doctor," requested her father as he dried his tears.

I looked down at her face which had enlightened many of my days and taught me what courage was all about. I leaned forward, kissed her forehead, and gently brought her eyelids together.

A few minutes later, I broke the news to her shaken husband.

"Why? Why God?" he kept repeating as he let his tears roll down his chest. "Why her? She's never hurt anyone in her life."

His mother-in-law got up and hugged him as his daughter tried to calm him down. He was falling apart.

"Mr. Smith, I need to ask you something," I said, fifteen minute later. "It's okay for you to refuse my request."

He looked up at me with his red, swollen eyes.

"I'm really sorry your wife died. You know how much I cared about her and also how I and all her other doctors were frustrated because we couldn't figure out what she had. She died with her secret hidden within her body and it's quite possible we might find out more about her disease if we had a chance to study it more. We might learn something from it and maybe even be able to help someone else in the future."

"You want her body?" he asked anxiously, as he looked at his father and mother-in-law.

"We told the doctor it's your decision, Mike. We want you to know we're supportive either way," his father-in-law said.

Mr. Smith cried for a while, dropping his head between his hands. Finally, he lifted it up and looked at me. "She loved you as her doctor ever since she first saw you with your Walt Disney tie. And you saw how much she suffered. Too much, doctor," he said, starting to cry again. "I never want to see another person go through what she went through, Dr. Baldi. If there's one chance in a hundred million you find something inside her body, something that will spare one person from suffering the way she did, then I give you her body. I entrust it to you. Go open it, look at it, learn from it, and I pray to God he guides your hand to discover her mysterious disease, not for our sake but for the sake of someone else in this world. She was always helpful to others and I'm sure she wants you to give your best care to future patients."

"God bless her soul," I replied.

I asked Dr. Bauer, the pathologist, if I could dissect her body and retrieve her organs. "No problem," he replied. It was the first time in years that a clinician asked him for such a favor.

We stood next to each other, dressed in long, plastic, butcher-like aprons. He handed me the tray with several sharp knives, scissors, and clamps. "Can I start?"

"Go right ahead. The jars are ready," he replied.

For the last time, I opened Mrs. Smith chest and belly. Her loving heart was still warm and her remaining intestines were moving around. I dissected her organs out and handed them one by one to Bauer, who briefly examined them before weighing them. He, too, had his knives, which he used to slice the organs before he finally dropped them inside his jars.

Silvia, who had helped me wheel Mrs. Smith down to the morgue, stood at the head of the bed and watched us as we desperately searched for the mysterious illness that had taken away a wonderful person, a loving wife, a caring mother, and an unforgettable patient.

- Thirty-seven -

"Professor Baldi, welcome to the Melstein service," the surgeon said as he shook my hand in the outpatient clinic. "Dr. Harshberg told me a lot about you."

"I'm looking forward to working with you the next two weeks," I replied.

"I heard you want to learn a little bit about plastic surgery."

"Yes, sir," I replied.

"Well, you came to right service. We do it all here. Boob job, facelift, liposuction, eyelids, nose reconstruction and everything in between."

"Sounds like a busy surgical service," I commented.

"Surgical service? Sometimes it feels more like a psychiatric ward," he joked. "You'll get to meet some of my crazy patients."

"Do you do anything other than cosmetics?"

He shook his head. "I used to. I spent twenty-five years of my life doing challenging reconstructive cases."

"Like what?"

"Car accidents, trauma, burns, kids born with screwed up faces and limbs. I've published over three hundred articles on reconstructive surgery."

"Why did you stop doing it?"

"Fame and reputation. The ACLS attracts rich people from all over the world and they all come here because they want to get operated by me."

"I see."

"They pay well for cosmetic surgery so the ACLS keeps encouraging them to come back and refer their friends to me. I don't mind meeting these people, it's just I hate spending all my days doing facelifts and sucking fat out of people's bellies," he replied with a smile. "My chief resident is on vacation, so it's just you and I. Let's go see the next patient."

We headed down the hallway until we reached the last room to the right. He grabbed the chart left outside the door, pulled the yellow sticker attached to it, and tossed it on the floor.

"What is it for?" I asked him pointing at the floor.

"A VIP sticker," he replied with disgust. "I hate it when the fuckin' ACLS flags my charts with these stickers. Why can't they understand that I treat all my patients the same?" he asked with a smirk. "I treat them all like shit!"

I couldn't help it but laugh.

"Shall we, professor?" he asked as he knocked on the door and opened it. "Good morning. I'm Dr. Melstein and this is my assistant Dr. Baldi," he introduced us.

"It's an honor to meet you," said the husband with a broken English accent as he got up to shake our hands.

"We heard a lot about you," added the wife, who was already dressed in a patient's gown. Half of her body was covered with expensive jewelry.

"I understand you came here from Columbia," he said.

"Yes, doctor."

"Aren't there any good plastic surgeons down there?"

"There are, but our cousin the president of Columbia recommended we come to you. You operated on his wife."

"Oh, yes, Mrs. Escobar!" He finally remembered her name.

"She was very happy with the final result," she complimented him.

He looked at me all proud. "Thank you," he replied. "Let's see now, you came here for a boob job," he said as he looked in her chart.

"Boob job?" she asked.

"Breast augmentation. To get them bigger," he tried to explain as he simulated with his hands two large breasts.

"Oh, yes," she replied.

"Did my nurse already explain to you the operation and its risks?"

"Yes, doctor."

"It's fairly simple. We cut your breasts open, stick a silicon and water implant under them, and we're finished. Really, it's a piece of cake," he explained in an insensitive manner.

"And the complications?"

"You won't get any," he replied arrogantly. She seemed concerned. "Well, sometimes people can get bleeding, infection, pain, the usual simple stuff. Don't worry, we can fix it for you," he continued in a derogatory fashion.

They were stunned by his comments. "Are you the surgeons who'll do it?" her husband asked in a defensive manner.

"Kind of. See, we'll work together but Dr. Baldi is a future radiologist. But really, there's nothing to worry about. Let's see," he said as he looked at her chart again. "You're scheduled in two days. Good, I guess I'll see you then," he commented as he got up and headed for the door.

"Doctor?" the woman hesitated to say. "Aren't you going to examine my chest?"

"Naah, not really. Just make sure you tell my nurse how big you want them," he replied as he quickly exited the room.

"Interesting couple," I commented nervously.

"Just like any other, wealthy and obnoxious," he replied. He laid the chart on the counter and started writing. "I never thought the day will come when my existence is reduced to a breast transplanter and a liposucker!" he added with a sarcastic smile.

"Sir?" I hesitated to say.

He looked at me. "What's that seriousness on your face all about?"

"No offense, sir, but these people came all the way from Columbia to see you and you were in the room with them for less than three minutes."

"Does it really matter how much time I spent with her? What truly matters is the good job I'll do on her chest."

"I understand, sir. But the way we talked to them must have confused them. She came to see a world renown plastic surgeon and now she thinks a radiologist is doing her surgery."

He laughed. "Don't you worry about it, even a shrink could do her surgery. Besides if she doesn't like the idea, she can go get it elsewhere. It's safer for us."

"Why?"

"Can you imagine if we fucked up her breasts? Mr. Escobar, her cousin, will come after us and kill us," he joked.

"You really think he would?" I asked him.

"Hell, yeah," he replied. "Let me tell you what happened to me once. About three years ago I did a face chemical peel on the wife of a gang leader from the northeast."

"Really?" I asked intrigued.

"The damn pharmacist forgot to dilute the acid so I poured the wrong liquid on her face and gave her a third degree burn. Her face was a big mess," he said as he watched the Colombian couple leave the room. "Good-bye now," he waved at them.

"What happened to the lady?"

"There was nothing I could do for her. I kept giving her the run-around until her husband nailed me one day in this room over there," he said as he pointed down the hallway. "He was very upset but he wasn't going to sue me. You know why?"

"Why?"

"He told me he had more money than God. Can you imagine?"

"That wealthy?"

"Yeah, he also told me to fix her face or else he was going to get me fixed!"

"What happened?"

"What do you think?" he asked as he grabbed his genitals. "He fixed me!"

"No shit?" I said, not knowing if I should believe him.

"Just kidding, son," he replied with a smile. "I finally told him the truth about the irreversible damage. I was really nervous he wasn't going to take it well."

"What did he do?"

"He asked me if there was anything else he could do. I don't know what got into me but I told him privately to get himself another woman."

"Did he get upset at you?"

"No, he laughed and did just like I told him."

"What?"

"The best part of it, I was the guest of honor at his wedding!"

- Thirty-eight -

"You look like shit," observed Melstein as we waited inside the operating room, while the nurses got Mrs. Glazer ready.

"There were a couple of trauma cases in the emergency room last night," I replied.

"Did you admit them to our service?" he asked.

"No, sir. I turfed them to orthopedics."

"You look kind of happy," commented Dr. Schonder, the anesthesiologist, as he looked at Melstein.

"I had a blast last night," he replied.

"What did you do?" he asked.

"I went to a cocktail party with my wife."

"How was it?"

"Great until my wife spoiled it for me."

"Really? Why did she?"

"Because I got drunk and started flirting with the young ladies," he replied with a laugh.

"Understandable," commented Carla, the scrub nurse. "Dr. Melstein, it's about time you start acting your age."

"I know," he replied. "That damn liquor always gets me in trouble. But I just love the taste of it."

"It seems you always go after young women," added Schonder.

"It's one of the five stages," he replied.

"What five stages?" I asked.

"Getting drunk. See, first you feel you're smart and you start talking to people about things you know nothing about. Second, you realize you're handsome, even when you're ugly, and you start flirting with the ladies. Third, you think you're rich, and you start buying drinks for people you've never met before. Fourth, you think you're invisible, and you start chasing ladies thinking your wife or girlfriend can't see you. And finally, you get this feeling of bulletproof immortality, and you feel you can get away with stupid things like driving a car drunk or jumping off a balcony without getting hurt."

"It seems you're always stuck at the fourth stage," joked Schonder.

"I'd lie if I said I didn't like young, pretty women," he admitted.

"You've got to be careful with these young women," Carla added.

"Speaking of which," he turned around and faced me, "did you know that someone researched the amount of bacteria shed by women of different ages inside the operating room?"

"Oh, no, not again!" said Carla. "You tell the story to every resident."

"One of the biggest studies ever. They found that young women shed less bacteria off their bodies than old ones," he said as he lifted his eyebrows. "But as usual, we do everything the wrong way in medicine. Instead of having young babes as surgical nurses, we get the old menopausal ones," he added joking. "For instance, why couldn't we get the pretty girls from physical therapy to help us up here? It would be better for both the patients and the surgeons!"

"Well, I'll be happy to leave anytime, Dr. Melstein," Carla threatened.

"You know I'm kidding," he continued, as he gave her a hug.

"Besides, if you really wanna talk about bacteria problems, just look at your big eyebrows," she fired back, pointing at his long, dandruff-plagued, gray eyebrows.

Schonder laughed his ass off.

"Speaking of bacteria, professor," he said as he looked at me, "do you believe much in this bacterial bullshit?"

"The germ theory, sir?"

He nodded.

"Of course, I do. The issue was settled about one hundred years ago. Germs and bacteria cause infections."

"You really think so?" he replied, discrediting my statement. "Son, the germ theory is all bullshit. It's over rated!"

"So you're saying what I learned in medical school was wrong?"

"If it was true, my eyebrows should have caused thousands of infections by now!"

"She's ready for you, doctors," commented Carla inviting us to go scrub our hands.

"You didn't meet Mrs. Glazer in the clinic because I saw her about a month ago," he said as he started washing his hands. "She came in with her husband for a facelift and liposuction of her belly and thighs."

"How old is she?"

"Seventy-eight and has twenty-one grandchildren."

"And she wants a facelift?" I asked in disbelief.

"What can I say, son? It's a vain society and it's only getting worse. She told me she'd rather spend the money on liposuction than give it to the grandchildren."

"And her husband agreed with that?"

"He was more worried about something else. Someone told him she was going to look as young as his daughter."

"And what did you tell him?" I asked.

He smiled. "I told him by the time I'm done with her she's going to look younger than his granddaughter!"

"How did he take it?"

"He felt like shit and now he wants liposuction. He's scheduled for next month."

"Is that right?"

"I'm going to melt his body because I'm the ultimate liposucker!" he replied with a French accent.

"What's with the accent, sir?" I was curious.

"Liposuction was invented by a Frenchman," he replied.

"Really? But I thought it was the most common operation performed in the United States."

"It is, but it was invented by a French obstetrician."

"Obstetrician?"

"Can you believe it? Everytime this doctor delivered a baby in Paris, he got disgusted by the fat his patients carried on their thighs and buttocks. One day, he thought about sticking a catheter into the fat and sucking it out. When he told his patients he was going to take their fat off for free, they lined up the hallway of his clinic by the dozens. Before he knew it, he had done over one thousand cases of liposuction without disclosing his invention to any other doctor."

"Why?"

"He wanted to make sure it worked. Then finally, he showed up one day to the International Congress of Plastic Surgery, dressed like a pimp with a leather jacket and a heavy gold necklace, and escorted by two young, beautiful women. It was scandalous."

"Is that right?"

"I guess it's the French way. You can only wonder how confused the plastic surgeons attending the conference were. They thought he was a lunatic," he said as he washed the soap off his arms and drained them. "However, soon after he showed them his videotape, they thought he was a genius."

"What was in the videotape?"

"It showed him inside an operating room with a face mask barely covering his mouth. He started talking about this fat lady on the table and about the metallic catheter he held in his hand. He called it a liposuction catheter and said he was going to stick it in her belly and suck out some fat. And that's exactly what he did. It was like a miracle watching the fat drip into the bucket on the floor. At the end of the tape, he turned around, pointed at the bucket and said something like *the fat goes into the bucket and this lady's money goes into my pocket!*"

"How interesting," I said.

"Within one week, he became the most famous doctor in the world and was awarded an honorary membership in the International Society of Plastic Surgery, an honor only bestowed on the most accomplished plastic surgeons of the century."

"Just because of liposuction," I said.

"Liposuction generates more money for plastic surgeons than any other procedure. You have to give the man some credit, even though he was just an obstetrician who hated fat ladies!"

"So he's a legend?"

"A unique one. Every year he returns to the International Congress escorted by a new group of gorgeous women and shares with the rest of us his continuing success in Paris."

"What a smart fellow," I commented.

"Smart? Naah, just lucky," he said as he opened the operating room door. "Come in, professor, let's suck some fat!"

"Where should I stand?" I asked.

"Go to the other side," he replied. He handed me a knife and a liposuction catheter.

"Sir, I've never done this before," I said, nervously.

"Don't worry. If an obstetrician can do it, you can do it," he replied, smiling. "There's nothing to it. Just look at how I'm doing it on this side and do your side the same way. Just stay horizontal with the catheter and stay away from shish kabobing her intestines."

He started and I imitated him. "How am I doing?" I asked, waiting for his approval.

"Great. Don't worry much about the bruising, they all get it."

"I'm actually enjoying this," I said.

"I told you plastics was easy. Even a shrink can do it!" he said, smiling. "And it pays well. A buttock or a thigh is about a grand in private practice. Just imagine, four thighs and a couple of bellies each morning, and you go play golf for the rest of the day with eight more grand in your bank account."

"Not bad for the amount of work."

"Not at all," he replied. "I can easily see you as a plastic surgeon, professor. Are you sure you wanna be a boring radiologist?"

"Pretty much, sir."

"Well, if you ever change your mind, there will always be a need for more liposuckers in this world!"

"I'll keep that in mind, sir."

"Carla, how much have we taken out so far?"

"About four liters," she answered after she leaned over and looked at the bag.

"I think we should stop here," he commented as he reached for my liposuction catheter. "Let's do her face now," he continued.

Carla brought two black, round stools to the head of the table. We each took one and sat on it.

"Did she have this done before?" I asked as soon as I noticed the scar behind her ears.

"Three times," he replied. "Why don't you grab your knife and cut your side the way I cut mine," he ordered me as he pushed her left ear forward and made one long incision down the back of her neck.

"Doctor, are you making it tight?" Mrs. Glazer asked in the middle of her facelift.

"Is she awake?" an angry Melstein asked.

"She's light on her sedation," Schonder replied. "I'll give her more."

"Now, take your small liposuction catheter and suck her neck fat evenly," he instructed me. "Good," he said as he saw me do it. "Just keep doing it the way you are."

He worked on her left side of the face as I did her right. Every now and then he glanced to make sure I was making good progress.

"What do you think?" I asked, pointing at her neck.

"Born to be a plastic surgeon!" he replied.

A few minutes went by. "Doctor, is my face tight enough?" she asked again.

"Schonder, what's the fuckin' deal? Shut her up," bitched Melstein.

"I'll give her more," he added.

"Be careful over there, professor," he warned, as he watched me dissect the neck. "There's a major nerve that goes there."

"Oops," I said, unaware of the possible damage I could inflict. "I sure don't wanna paralyze her face."

"You've done well so far. Just start closing the deep layer with some Vicryl sutures," he ordered.

Nervous, I slowly closed the deep muscles of her neck.

Fifteen minutes later, he was almost done with his side. "How is it coming over..."

"Doctor, did you make my face tight enough? I want it tight, very tight," she mumbled again.

Melstein wasn't too thrilled to hear her voice another time. He slapped the surgical table with his hand. "Listen to me, Mrs. Glazer, I made your face so tight, your pubic hair is sitting under your chin right now!"

Everyone laughed except me. "Sir, the patient is awake..."

"Don't worry, professor, she isn't going to remember any of this."

"Yeah, he's right," Schonder said. "She's heavily sedated now. Just continue your work, gentlemen."

"What time is it?" asked Melstein, as he proceeded to finish sewing her left side.

"Quarter to twelve," Carla replied.

"I can't miss lunch," he said, stepping away from the table. "Just finish your side and join me upstairs."

"Sir, do you want to check to see if I connected her ear to her face correctly?" I tried to catch him before he stepped into the hallway.

"Naah, not really. I do trust you, professor," he replied with a smirk. "Besides, even if you fuck up, you can't make her any uglier than she was!"

- Thirty-nine -

Although I enjoyed working with Dr. Melstein, I missed the Harshberg service. After many cases of liposuction, boob jobs, and facelifts, I returned to the cardiovascular team.

"Guess who's back again?" Harshberg asked.
"Who?"
"Your friend, Joe Merck."
"No shit!"
"The man is never going to die," he said, shaking his head.
"I guess, sir, you keep saving his life."
"No, son. I don't keep saving his life. The truth is that Satan doesn't want the bastard. Each time Merck has a close brush with death, Satan dumps him back on me."
"Why is he back this time?"
"His right leg is infected. His family doctor called me earlier this morning and transferred him over here."
"Are we cutting him again?"
"I don't think we have a choice. His leg has to come off this time. It's either that or his life."
"This will be his fifth operation in six months. Do you think his weak heart will be able to handle it?"
"At this point, I'm not even afraid of a heart attack or a stroke," Harshberg said, adjusting his cowboy hat. "We have put him through hell already and his shitty heart has done well."

"Good morning, Joe," Harshberg said, as we entered his room. "I brought Dr. Baldi with me."
Merck looked bad. "I'm hurtin'. I can't take this any longer," he moaned.
"We're here to help you, if you're willing to listen to us this time," continued Harshberg.
"Can't you just take care of my pain?" Merck pleaded.
"Your pain is beyond pain killers and antibiotics. We need to do more this time," Harshberg responded.
"You don't mean surgery again?" he said, as he lifted his head up and looked at me.
"Joe, God knows how hard I've tried to save your leg in the past," Harshberg responded softly. "Your clogged blood vessels

are the worst I've ever seen and I'm afraid your only option now is to get rid of that leg."

"Amputate it? No fuckin' way, doc."

"I'm afraid so. We need to cut it off just above the knee."

"I would rather die than lose my leg. Just give me some pain killers and leave me alone. My leg will heal by itself."

"Joe, I don't think you understand how serious the situation is. We're not talking about pain here, we're talking about your life. Your leg needs to come off."

"What if I refuse to have the operation?"

"It's your right to refuse it as long as you understand your life is in danger and you may die within a week or two."

"What do you think, Dr. Baldi? Should I have the operation?"

"I agree with Dr. Harshberg. Your leg needs to come off."

"You're not saying that because you're still mad at me for setting you up on that blind date? You're not trying to get rid of me, are you?" he said forcing himself to smile.

"Not at all, sir."

"So what do you say?" Harshberg asked him.

"I'll have it under one condition. After you cut off my leg, I want you to give it to my daughter."

"And why would you want me to do that?" Harshberg asked, raising his eyebrows in surprise.

"She'll drive it to the mortuary to get it cremated," he replied. "When I die, I want the rest of my body cremated as well and added to my leg."

"Why is it so important to you?"

"I know that I'll be reborn as an angel and I certainly don't want to be flying around missing a leg!"

"Really?" I asked not knowing if I should laugh.

"I'm afraid I can't honor your request," replied Harshberg. "It's against the law to hand out body parts."

"It's my leg."

"I understand that," Harshberg added. "But can you imagine if people drove around with body parts?"

"I should be free to do whatever I want with my leg," he insisted.

"So you won't have the surgery?"

"Not unless you do as I told you."

"How about if I ask someone from the mortuary to come by and pick it up?" Harshberg asked.

"As long as I don't have to pay for it!" he answered.

"Done deal. I'll ask the hospital to pay for it and even if they don't, I'll pay for it myself," he replied, triumphantly. "So you agree to the operation then?"

"One more request," he added. "Tell the nurse to give me back my cigarettes."

"You know your cigarettes got you in trouble in the first place," he hurried to reply.

"I don't care. I know I'm going to die with a cigarette in my hand."

"If that's what you truly want, you can have them back," he replied unconvinced. "I guess it's too late to make you quit now."

"When do you want to cut it off?" he asked.

"You're on the schedule for tomorrow," Harshberg replied. "Make sure you rest well."

"So, what do you think?" Harshberg asked me, as he opened Merck's chart.

"About what?" I replied.

"Flying with the angels," he said, smiling. "Joe doesn't need a cardiovascular surgeon, he needs a fuckin' shrink!"

"I could have told you that a long time ago. Hopefully, it's the last time we see him, sir."

"I'm not sure about that anymore. The way things are going, I may get my heart attack before his," he said, with a smile, then took out his black pen and wrote in the chart:

Patient is well known to me as I have already cut him four times. He is a pathetic man crying in his misery and asking for his cigarettes. His right lower extremity ischemia has progressed. He has a gangrenous and infected extremity. His only option now is a right above knee amputation. I have discussed with him risks, goals, and alternatives in detail. He understands and wishes to proceed tomorrow morning.
Willie Harshberg, M.D.

- Forty -

"Hospital operator. How can I help you?" It was a soft, sweet voice that I had become used to hearing every night.
"Dr. Baldi, here," I replied. "Can I request a wake up call at five o'clock?"
"No problem, sir. I hope you'll get some sleep. You sound very tired."
"We had a killer day. I can definitely use some rest."
"It seems you're always in the hospital working."
"It's surgical internship. That's how it's meant to be, busy and painful."
"How much longer do you have with us?" she inquired.
"One more month."
"And then?"
"Back to California."
"Really? Where?" She sounded a bit curious.
"Palo Alto. I have a job in the radiology department at Stanford University."
"Is work as hard over there?"
"It's a piece of cake compared to the Harshberg service. This is as brutal as it gets."
"I bet you can't wait to get over there."
"I'm not really sure about that."
"What do you mean?"
"I'll miss this service," I replied. "The patients, the operating room, Dr. Harshberg's harassment, Dr. Ungaman, and all the excitement I had this year. There's never a dull day on the Harshberg service. Every day is full of action."
"Just like in Hollywood," she replied.
"Except it's real stuff."
"I see," she said. "Well, doctor, I hope you rest well tonight."
"I hope so, too," I replied. "By the way, I've always wondered about where the operator is located."
"A small room on top of the hospital."
"Really?" I asked. "Are you always there by yourself?"
"Usually. The security guard checks on me every now and then."
"Do you ever get lonely up there?"
"Sometimes. But I have a beautiful view of the city. The lights, the buildings, the streets, I can see it all."

"How do you keep busy?"

"I read and listen to music when I'm not paging doctors or talking to patients."

"Is it hard to talk to people you've never met?"

"Not really. It's just a job for me," she replied with her young, friendly voice.

"For how long have you been doing it?"

"Three years."

"Are you going to do it for the rest of your life?"

"I don't think so. But for now I'm happy."

"I see," I replied. "You really have a beautiful voice," I commented.

"Thank you, doctor," she replied. "Your accent is wonderful, too."

I felt very flattered. It was the nicest thing I'd heard in a while. "You're really sweet for saying that," I replied.

"Well, I better let you go to sleep," she said nervously. "Good night, doctor."

"Wait," I hurried to say. "Do you have to go? Is someone else calling?" I asked her. Suddenly, I was eager to know more about her.

"Not really."

"Do you mind if we talked a bit more?"

"Not at all, it's just I thought you needed your rest," she responded politely.

"I do. But I haven't talked to someone for a long time."

"Really? It's hard to imagine that, especially since you must carry a hundred conversations a day with your patients and colleagues."

"I do, but it's all work related," I admitted. "It's nice to talk about something else every now and then."

"I see," she said and then went quiet.

"Well... How's the view from up there?"

"Beautiful, especially when it snows."

"Do you ever get cold in the winter time?"

"I have a little heater next to my desk and I always make myself a cup of hot chocolate," she said.

"How romantic!"

"So, doctor..." I felt the nervousness in her voice. "Do you like the doctors you work with?" she said, changing the subject.

"I do. Especially Dr. Harshberg and Dr. Ungaman."

"What is Dr. Harshberg like? Is he as bad as I hear?"

"The guy is a cowboy, he's tough, rough, and takes no shit from anyone."

"Really?"

"But he can say funny and hilarious things at times."

"Like what?"

"Like today, he argued with me about the human body. He tried to convince me that the intestines are more important than the brain. He said that a person can live without a brain but not without intestines."

"Is that right?"

"Yeah, he cited modern politicians as an example to illustrate his point. In Harshberg's opinion, politicians are brainless but they have the guts to break the law and get away with it!"

"How funny! And how about Dr. Ungaman?"

"His sex drive is in his knife. If life for William Shakespeare was to be or not to be, for Cutter Ungaman it is to cut or not to cut, that is his question!"

She giggled then asked if Cutter was married.

"Why do you ask?"

"Just wondering..."

"Wondering about what?"

"He's awfully nice to me over the telephone. Sometimes, I even sense that he likes me."

I laughed. "That's Cutter. He's married but he's always looking around."

"No offense, doctor, but all men are the same."

"Not true," I replied. "Some men are destined for one woman."

"You truly believe that?" she asked.

"Absolutely. They just have to find their lost half. Sometimes they do, and sometimes they don't. See, love..."

"I hate to interrupt you, doctor, but the other phones are ringing."

"Oh... Okay," I replied, disappointed to end the conversation prematurely. "I guess we can talk another time."

"I'd really like that, Dr. Baldi. You know where to find me."

- Forty-one -

"Go home, Cutter," Harshberg ordered. "I know you hate to miss the opportunity to cut, but your wife is sick and she needs you. Go be with her."

"Okay. I'll see you in the morning," he replied, somewhat disappointed to miss the last case of the day.

"So, Rastus, it's you and I on this one," Harshberg said.

"I guess so, sir."

"Well, the year is drawing to an end and I think it's about time we do a case together without Cutter. Not that I don't like operating with him. I just wanted this case to be yours since Joe is your friend. You've known him from the beginning and it's only fair that you take his leg off."

"I'll be honored to do it, sir," I replied.

"I knew you would be," he said. "You know, Rastus, we should have amputated his leg a long time ago. I just don't know why I tried so hard to save it."

"Sometimes, one isn't sure, sir."

"I was sure, Rastus. Legs like his always end up in the bucket," he replied. "In any case, he's getting today what has been long due," he continued. "Have you ever assisted on an amputation?"

"I've seen one in medical school."

"Do you remember any of it?"

"Vaguely, sir. But I know the fishmouth procedure very well."

"How come?" he asked surprised.

"I read it in the surgery textbook over lunch break today," I said.

Harshberg laughed. "So you like to read, Rastus? You sure do amaze me sometimes," he said, shaking his head. "Let's go do it," he added, as he drained the water off his arms and then walked into OR seven.

Ron welcomed us. "Doctors, you look like two priests ready to conduct a religious mass," he said, referring to the way we held our arms up in the air before we got gowned.

"Well, Ron," Harshberg said, "it may very well turn into a mass, to be exact a funeral, especially since Dr. Baldi is the one to be cutting today!"

"I better get some classical music then," Ron suggested.

"The only classical I want to listen to is classical country," he joked as he stood on the opposite side of the table. "Knife to Dr. Baldi," he requested.

"Here you go, Dr. Baldi," Inger said as she handed me the knife.

I held it in my hand for a while and hesitated.

"Go ahead, son," Harshberg encouraged me. "Don't get scared by the knife, it's your best friend," he added. "Back in the civil war, you saved a man's life by amputating his leg. It was true back then and it's still true today. Joe is your friend and he needs your help, so go ahead."

Reluctantly, I pushed the knife against Merck's skin and started cutting. "Sorry, Joe," I said.

After a few minutes, Harshberg sat down on a black stool and leaned his back against the wall. "You're on your own, son. Let's see how much you remember from that textbook of yours."

Nervously, I proceeded with the cutting until I finally reached his bone. Inger took away the knife and handed me a thin saw. I grabbed it with my shaking hands and looked at Harshberg. He gave his approval. I started sweating. Although it took less than a minute to cut Joe's leg off, it seemed like eternity. Finally, it dropped on the table.

"To the bucket, son," Harshberg ordered, as I held the leg with both of my hands. "To the bucket because that's where it belongs."

"What should I use for closure?" I asked.

"Gut chromic," he replied.

Inger handed me what I needed and I got busy closing his wound.

"Tighter, son. You need to make these stitches tighter," he ordered.

"I'm trying my best, sir," I replied.

"No, Rastus, you're not trying your best unless I hear you let out a couple of farts each time you tie!"

Gastein laughed. "So, is Merck going to become a frequent flyer at the ACLS?"

"Well, let's see," replied Harshberg as he counted his fingers. "We can do his other leg, his belly, his heart, his aorta, and his brain arteries... The opportunities with him are endless!"

"I'm sure you'd like to see him again," I said.

"What makes you think that?" Harshberg asked.

"No offense, sir, but he seems to be one of the very few patients you have ever really cared about..."

"Are you implying that I'm not a caring doctor?" Harshberg interrupted.

"Well, not exactly, sir. I just meant..."

"I understand what you meant and you're right. I can be quite insensitive at times," he admitted. "But that's part of being a cardiovascular surgeon, son. The tragedies we see are swords with double edges. They teach us lessons and improve our technical skills but also they harden our hearts. And that's a reality we must accept," he continued.

"Hum..."

"Sensitivity always destroys a surgeon's concentration," he added. "When I have a man on my table dying on me because of a ruptured aorta, I can't afford to be emotional. I can't think about his loving wife, children, and grandchildren crying in the hallway outside my operating room. My thoughts are with my hands, my knife, and my pair of scissors because that's the only way I can save some of these people and pull them through their catastrophes."

He paused. I didn't know how to respond to his comment.

"But it's true that I carry my insensitivity with me outside the operating room," he continued. "It's tragic not to be able to feel with one's heart at times but for me there's no way around it," he added. "Now, let me ask you a question. If you were sick and in need of a surgeon, would you rather have one to cut you and fix you, or one to hold your hand?"

"To cut me and fix me, of course," I replied, as I looked at him.

"We need then not discuss it further. Now, to answer your question about Merck, I admit that I care about the bastard. And my feelings are purely selfish. He means something to me because he's the ultimate cardiovascular patient. Surgeons like me spend their entire careers trying to meet characters like him. He's what makes my life fun and exciting. I treat many patients with cardiovascular disease but seldom do I come across a patient with both the disease and the personality trait. Mr. Merck is not only a medical challenge, he's a mental case! His passive-aggressive, self-destructive, fatalistic, yet funny, and witty personality make him very special. In many way, he's just like a good cardiovascular surgeon: a fighter and a survivor."

- Forty-two -

I'd been looking forward to calling the hospital operator all day. "I hope I'm not interrupting you, " I said, when she answered the phone.
"Not at all, Dr. Baldi," she replied, her voice as sweet as ever.
"Please call me Mick," I promptly added.
"How have you been?" she asked.
"Pretty good. A few ups and downs."
"So... You're leaving us next week?"
"It's hard to believe it, but internship is almost over."
"You're going to California... It must be beautiful over there," she commented.
"You've never been there?"
"I've only seen it in the movies."
"Maybe you should come and visit sometime," I added.
"Maybe, but I have to save some money first," she replied.
"Well... I'm going to miss our late night conversations," I hesitated to say.
"I really enjoyed them, too," she replied sincerely. "You're a nice person, Dr. Baldi."
I was flattered. "Mick. Please call me, Mick," I reminded her. "Ugh... I feel really embarrassed, but I've never asked for your name."
"Melodie. I'm Melodie Fabella."
"What kind of a name is Fabella?"
"Italian."
"Is that where you're from?"
"I was born in Guatemala, but my father originally came from Italy."
"I see. Does Fabella mean anything?'
"Beautiful. At least that's what my dad told me a long time ago."
"Fabella," I said, modulating my voice. "I like how it sounds."
"Thank you."
"So... Are you close to your dad?"
"I was."
"And now?"
"He died three years ago."

"I'm sorry to hear that. Was he old?"
"Sixty-two," she sadly replied. "He was a nice man."
"I'm sure he was."
"He was a doctor, too."
"Really?"
"He went to medical school in Italy but did his residency in Guatemala. That's where he met my mother."
"What did he die of?"
"Cancer."
"I hope he didn't suffer."
"He did."
"I'm sure your mother made it easier for him."
"She left him when she learned he had cancer," she responded. "I stayed home with him for a year."
"I'm sure he appreciated that."
"I couldn't turn my back on him or put him in a hospice. He took great care of me as a little girl and I felt it was only fair I do the same for him."
"It must have been hard taking care of him by yourself."
"The hardest part was dealing with his depression. He felt betrayed by my mother."
"I can only imagine. Were they having much trouble together?"
"On the contrary, my parents were madly in love."
"And she left him?" I inquired. "It's hard to believe."
"I know it's hard to understand. But she couldn't be with him."
"And their love?"
"That was the problem. My mother couldn't accept the fact he was dying in her front of her eyes. She ran away before things got out of hand for him. She wanted to remember only the good memories."
"Strange way of looking at it."
"I know, but different people love differently," she replied. "I don't blame my mother for what she did, especially after what I saw my father go through. The last three months of his life were horrible. He'd lost his mind, he was incontinent most of the time and was no longer the intelligent and compassionate person he was. He just wasn't the same at the end."
"You loved him?"
"I still do."
"And you stayed with him?"

"I did."
"Your mother should have, too."
"I'm not sure she should have."
"I can only imagine how betrayed he felt."
"At the end, he couldn't remember anything."
"Still, it's an awful thing to watch your loved one walk away from you."
"I know, but his suffering ended with his death. My mother's pain will never end."
"I never thought about it that way. Would you do what your mother did if you were in her shoes?"
"I can't answer that. I've never been in love."
"Suppose you were madly in love with someone. Would you do what she did?"
"I don't know. But having seen what my dad went through, I'm not sure I could go through it again."
"What would you do?"
"I'd probably kill myself," she replied in a serious tone. "But again, I'm just supposing."
"Supposing what?"
"That I were madly in love."
"Would you really kill yourself?"
"Most likely."
"You're unusual."
"Unusual?" she repeated.
"You'd kill yourself for a man?"
"If I loved him that much, what meaning would life have after him?"
"You can always find another man."
"Yeah, but it's not the same."
"You know, many people remarry."
"Other people can do whatever they like," she responded. "I see marriage as a one time deal. You can have a good fortune or a bad one, but you can only have one. I believe in getting dealt one set of cards in life, a winning set or a loosing one. But you don't get two."
"You believe in this?"
"It's the only thing that makes sense to me, Mick."
"You're really special, you know that?"

- Forty-three -

Two-thirty in the morning and the hallways were fully deserted. Restless, I wandered from ward to ward trying to soothe my aching soul. An occasional snore reminded me of the hundreds of patients occupying the rooms of the ACLS. After pacing several of the floors back and forth, I landed in the physicians lounge, where my exhausted body collapsed on the couch. But I couldn't fall asleep. I needed to talk this problem out. So I reached over to the telephone and slowly dialed his beeper number. I knew that he wouldn't take long to answer. I hung up and kept my hand on the receiver. Sure enough, it rang before I had time to catch some sleep.

"Dr. Ungaman, cardiovascular surgery. I was paged to this number," he said, in a barely audible voice. It was obvious he was still half-asleep.

"Hi. This is Mick. Sorry to wake you."

"What's up?"

"Well...." I hesitated.

"Well, what?" he asked, clearly impatient. "Is Mr. Stone Okay?"

Stone was one of the sickest patients on the service. He had his chest cracked for the fourth time the day before.

"Yeah, he's cruising nicely through the night," I replied.

"Then who's sick?" he asked, his voice now in full boom.

"It's me," I cried out. "And this damn internship."

"Shiiit. Did you kill somebody?"

"Nobody's dead. Not yet anyhow," I replied, bitterly.

"Then what Mick?"

"Well..." I stuttered.

"What?"

"I'mmm..."

"YOU'RE A FUCKIN' ASSHOLE!" he shouted. "You wake me up in the middle of the goddamn night just to mumble a few words. What's the fuckin' matter with you tonight? Grab them balls of yours and squeeze hard. Maybe you'll spit out a few words!"

"CUTTER!"

"Yeeaah," he moaned over the telephone.

"Don't talk to me like this."

"You stop mumbling for once and I'll stop," he paused for a short while. "Now, I'm gonna ask you one more time before I hang up on you, what's fuckin' wrong?"

"I'm confused."

"Confused? You woke me up to tell me that you're CONFUSED," he exclaimed. "I already knew that."

"No. I mean really confused."

"Oh, really? And what's confusing you?"

"I don't know. Nothing makes sense anymore."

"What doesn't make sense?" he said, sarcastically. "You're done, man. Two more days, forty-eight more hours and you're history. Out the door."

"That's exactly the problem. I don't think I'm ready to leave."

"What? You're not ready to leave. Let me tell you something, you little shit. Two more days and Harshberg is getting rid of you."

"I can't leave, Cutter. I'm in love." There. I finally admitted it.

"In love?" He was caught by surprise. "Kari? I thought you'd gotten over the bitch."

"She's not a bitch," I felt compelled to say. "In any case, it's someone else."

"No shit? And who's the lucky recipient of your holy fuck... I meant holy love?"

"The hospital operator. I'm in love with her."

"You're in love with the hospital operator? You're shitting me, Mick. You must be shitting me..."

"Why would I?"

"Because you're full of shit. That's why."

"Cutter, I love her."

"Are you fuckin' serious?"

"Serious like a deadly heart attack," I replied.

A few seconds later he was on the other line. His wife, who was awakened by the call, slammed down the phone in their bedroom. "You, dummshit. How come you haven't told me any of this before?" He demanded a full explanation.

"I wasn't sure."

"How long has this been going on?"

"I don't know."

"What in the fuck do you know? You wake me up in the middle of the goddamn night just to tell me that you don't know. I'm running out of patience you son of a bitch!"

"Calm down, Cutter. I called you for help."
"Start telling me what you know then."
"I love her. I miss her. I can't live without her. I can't leave her, the way things are..."
"Is she pregnant?"
"No chance of that," I said. "We've never met."
"What? You never met her?"
"Never."
"Mick, this ain't bullshit?"
"Honest to God."
"How can you be in love with someone you never met?"
"We've been talking over the phone for the last month. You know, when I'm up on night duty. I love listening to her voice."
"Voice? Voices can fool you."
"Maybe. But she has the most romantic voice I'd ever heard in my life." She had the voice of an angel.
"You watch opera, Mick?"
"What does that have to do with anything?"
"The big fat ladies have romantic voices, too!" he laughed.
"Thanks, Cutter. I thought that you were my friend. I called you for help. Good night."
"Wait. Don't hang up. I don't mean to hurt your feelings. You know that I was joking," he said, softening his tone. "I care about you, Mick."
"Sure you do, you little bastard."
I was as guilty playing passive-aggressive as he was.
"I just don't want you to get hurt. You're leaving in two days. Why can't you wait 'til California to fall in love. I hear it's nursing heaven out there. You can meet lots of them."
"It's not a matter of meeting people."
"Look, Mick. I don't want you to do something you might regret. Internship can do weird things to otherwise rational people. Believe me, I know from personal experience. Just don't let it push you into fantasy land."
"I'M NOT FANTASIZING," I fired back.
"Come on, Mick. Be reasonable. You've never met the girl. Do you know how old she is?"
"Stop calling her a girl!"
"How old is she?"
"I don't know."
"Under eighteen. For sure..." he guessed.
Our conversation wasn't going anywhere. Cutter and I weren't talking at the same level. Why should we? He was the

BEYOND THE MAGIC SCALPEL • 167

chief resident. I was the intern. He was married to a neurotic wife who drove him crazy. I was a bachelor, free to romance as many of the nurses in the hospital as I desired. At times it bugged him. But the only excitement left in his boring life came from listening to my dating stories. Through the eyes of his young intern he fantasized about the single life he never had. Cutter married his high school sweetheart --nothing sweet was left about her now-- in his freshman year of college.

"I'm sorry I called you. I don't know what I was expecting from you, Cutter."

"It's okay. We all need someone to talk to sometime. Do you really love her?"

"Yeah. She's really special. She says beautiful things."

"Like what?"

"Love is sacred. She's willing to die for it."

"What else has she told you? Any sex stuff?" He was obviously dying to hear some details.

"What's the matter with you, married doc?" I shot back. "You always seem more interested in my sex life than yours!"

"Marriage sucks, brother."

"Then get out of it."

"I wish I could, Mick. But you know my wife is a lawyer."

Poor Cutter was stuck in a marriage he didn't really want. The saddest part of it was that he was a good looking fellow and almost every nurse at the ACLS, single or married, wanted him on any given day. His southern sex appeal, they say, was irresistible.

"So tell me, any phone sex?"

"No, Cutter. The girl is pure and innocent."

"Right. Right. So what have you been talking about? The goddamn weather? The shitty cafeteria food?"

"None of your business, Cutter."

"Hell, it is! You woke me up in the middle of the night. It's my business."

"I called to ask for your advice."

"Me, who do you think I am? Your fuckin' priest?"

"Cutter, should I go up there and meet her?"

He paused for a while. "Naah. Just keep it a phone romance."

"I may miss out on meeting a princess."

"The princess of 'Whales'?" he joked.

"Way to spoil it Cutter. The way I see it, she's up in a tower waiting for her prince intern to discover her."

"You still believe in fairy tales?"
"Don't you?"
"I believe that you're a crazy son of a bitch. But that's what I love about you."
"So, Should I do it?"
"I guess. What do you have to lose at this point? The rest of your hair? You're bald already as it is!"

- Forty-four -

With sixteen hours left in my internship year, I found myself standing on the terrace outside Melodie's room. Although I had never met her before, her kind and sweet words had ignited my desire to pursue her further. But the thought of emotional rejection made me feel weak in the knees as I struggled to walk up the emergency stairs to the top of the hospital where she worked.

After several minutes of insecurity, hesitation and pounding heart beats, I knocked on her door. I was prepared for a surprise, even if it meant a big disappointment.

"Oh... Hi, Dr. Baldi," she said with a warm, welcoming smile.

I was surprised that she recognized me before hearing my voice. I stared at her beautiful green eyes for a moment. "Melodie?" I finally uttered. "Are you Melodie?"

"Yes, doctor," she replied, as she gently pushed back her long, silky, golden hair, behind her ears.

"Please call me Mick."

"Would you like to come in?" she asked, as she showed me the way into the small office that barely had enough room to fit a keyboard switch and a few phones.

"How did you recognize me?" I inquired, taking a seat on a small chair next to her.

"The hospital and physicians directory," she replied, pointing at a thick book sitting to the right of her desk. "Your picture is in there."

"I see."

"Besides, I read your name tag."

"Oh... yes," I said, as I nervously touched the small wooden piece pinned to my chest.

"I must admit, I'm really surprised to see you in person," she said.

Her physical beauty was breathtaking. Her pretty, slightly-curved nose crowning her thin, adorable lips was the work of a delicate sculptor.

"Well... It's my last night of duty..." I said, searching hard for the appropriate words.

"And?" she tried to encourage me.

"I thought I'd come up here and take a look at the beautiful view you told me about."

"Here, it is," she replied, as she pointed to the city fantastically displayed on the other side of her large glass window. "Is it the way you imagined it?"

"Even better than you described."

"I always feel as if I were flying in a plane and slowly landing in the city," she continued. "It's too bad we can't see the stars and the moon tonight. But on a night with a clear sky, it's a heavenly view from up here," she said, with a romantic overtone.

"Heavenly, it is," I echoed, fully captivated by her very seductive green eyes.

"Yeah," she responded. "The Italians would say, *a fa morire.*"

"What does it mean?"

"Something to die for."

"Most definitely," I replied nodding my head. "Most definitely."

"Why are you looking at me like that?" she asked, with a nervous smile.

"I'm just surprised."

"By what?"

"You're not the way that I imagined you."

"How did you imagine me?"

I thought for a bit and then laughed.

"What's the matter?" she asked, concerned.

"Nothing really," I continued. "I just remembered a conversation I had with Dr. Ungaman earlier tonight."

"About me?"

I hesitated. "Yeah... We wondered about what kind of a person would do your kind of night job," I said. "He bet you were a BFW."

"BFW?"

"It stands for big fat whale," I replied. "I'm sure he was teasing me."

"I see," she smiled. "Well, I'm sorry if my looks disappointed your imagination."

"Not at all. I'm delighted to see how wrong his prediction was," I replied. "How old are you?"

"Twenty-three," she answered.

"Why this job?" I inquired.

"It's not a bad job, you know."

"I'm sorry, I didn't mean it the way it sounded."
"How did you mean it?"
"You're so beautiful and there are so many other things you can do with your life."
"I'm doing them," she jumped in.
"Really?"
"I'm at the University in the afternoons working on a sociology degree. Since my father died, this job is the only way I can support myself and pay for my education."
"Didn't he leave you any money?"
"He did, but his illness consumed most of it. His medical insurance didn't cover half of his medical bills for one reason or another. People in the insurance business are a bunch of crooks," she replied angrily. "He donated his real estate to charity after his death. I encouraged him to do that."
"But how about you?"
"You know when my father came from Italy, he had nothing except for his education. I want to start my life the same way he did. There's no shame in being poor," she replied, with pride. "You know what he used to tell me about money?"
"What?"
"It can often bring you poverty of the soul."
"He must have been a very special person."
"You remind me of him."
"Do I?"
"You both have the same accent. Where are you from?"
"I'm Mediterranean, too. From Lebanon."
"It's a special part of the world."
"Have you been there?"
"No. My dad had promised to take me for a whole year to tour the Mediterranean countries when I was old enough. He died before it happened."
"Maybe one day."
"Maybe, but I have to visit California first," she said, smiling.
"You must. You can live with me if you come," I replied enthusiastically.
"Live with you?" she asked, surprised.
"I meant, you can be my guest if you came," I said, clarifying my words, not my underlying feelings for her.
"You're very kind," she replied with a sincere, loving face.
After a few minutes of silence I decided it was time to leave. "You have things to do," I said, as I got up to leave.

"You don't have to leave if you don't want to, Mick," she replied, a bit disappointed.

"I came up here to see the view and it's very beautiful... Just as you described it," I said, and extended my hand for a shake.

A cloud of sadness came across her face. "You're a very special doctor, you know," she said, as she shook my hand, gently drawing me towards her. "Your patients have said many nice things about you throughout the past year. You'll be missed around here."

"Thank you," I replied. "You made my life much easier by listening to me over the telephone. Good-bye, Melodie."

"Good-bye," she said, letting go of my hand. She seemed discouraged by my premature departure.

"Melodie?" I asked as I turned around to face the door.

"Yeah?" she replied.

"Have you ever kissed a man up here before?"

"No."

"Would you like to kiss one?"

"Who?" she asked.

"Someone who deeply cares about you and dreams about you often. Someone who's eager to touch your hand. Would you?"

"I would tell him many things," I heard her voice from behind me.

"Like what?" I asked still facing the door with my hand on the handle.

"I would tell him that I've liked him ever since I heard his accent over the telephone about a year ago. I would tell him that I sneaked into the emergency room many nights and watched him work from far away. I would tell him that I love him as much as he loves me. I would confess that I never had the courage to tell him that because he's a doctor and I'm just a hospital operator," she said and paused. "I would also tell him that he's a big fool if he walks out of this room without kissing me."

"Are you talking to me?"

"I'm talking to Mick Baldi, if he's still in the room."

I turned around. She was standing with her arms wide open and ready to absorb all the love and affection I could give her.

- Forty-five -

"Cutter, look at Rastus," Harshberg said.
"I'm looking," he replied as he stared at me.
"Is there something different about him this morning?"
"I don't know, sir."
"He's a happy man. And you know why, Cutter?"
"No, sir."
"It's his last day on my service," Harshberg replied with a smile. "The son of a bitch can't wait to leave!"
"It's up to you, sir. You can keep him another year if you'd like," he said, with a wink of an eye.
"Rastus, you've been counting the hours, haven't you?"
"No, sir."
"You're a pathologic liar, son," he said, shaking his head. "Are you telling me that you'd spend another year on my service?"
"If I had to, I would."
"And if you didn't have to, would you volunteer?"
"On your service, sir?"
"On my service, unless of course, you'd rather spend a whole year with Dr. Schinstein."
"No, sir."
"No, sir, what?"
"No, I would shoot myself in the leg before I'd go to his service."
"So you'd come back to my service?"
"Only if Cutter stays, sir."
"Cutter, what do you say?"
"Most willing, sir," he replied, enthusiastically. "I think I can handle a few more aortas!"
"I hate to admit it, boys, but you were a winning team," he said, adjusting his cowboy hat.
"Thank you, sir," we both replied.
"You'll be missed," Harshberg said sincerely. "You're leaving me with lots of good memories."
"I'll never forget your service," Cutter added.
"So are you set for next year?" Harshberg asked Cutter.
"Yes, sir, just as planned. I'm heading West to do my pediatric surgery fellowship."
"You're really interested in kids?"

"Yes, sir. I want to operate on the little sick ones."

"Well, Dr. Ungaman, you were an exemplary chief resident. Your eagerness to cut and heal was inspirational and you've completed your year with great honors. I have no doubt you'll be one of the best pediatric cardiac surgeons in this country."

"Thank you for your confidence, sir."

"Please do keep in touch and if I can be of any help to you in finding a job in the future, just let me know. I know a lot of people in this country. But quite honestly, I'm hoping you'll come back to the ACLS one day and fill my shoes."

"Thank you, sir," he replied.

"You're free to go, son. God bless you," Harshberg said, as he extended his right hand for a shake.

Cutter stood at military attention as he shook his hand. "It was an honor, sir," he said before taking off.

"Well, Rastus..."

"Sir?"

"Are you in a hurry?"

"Not really, sir."

"Let's go to the Espresso Bar and grab some coffee."

"Most willing, sir."

We quickly walked through the ward and took the stairs down to the coffee stand, near the emergency room.

"What would you like to drink?" he asked me.

"What are you having?"

"A double Espresso."

"Make it two," I said, to the lady who made the coffee.

"It's a beautiful day outside. Let's go sit over there," he suggested, pointing to the garden just opposite to the cafeteria. "Rastus, I was very pleased with your overall performance. You did a good job on my service and I want to thank you for taking care of all my patients."

"Thank you, sir. I enjoyed the experience," I replied, politely.

"My service is probably one of the toughest in this country. You survived it for a whole year and that tells me alot about how well you'll do in the future."

"Thank you, sir."

"My patients appreciated what you did for them. It may not have seemed that way, but all of them truly did. When they're in the hospital, they're usually too sick to express themselves. But believe me, a lot of them will ask for you when they come back to the clinic. For them, you're the doctor. They don't see who cuts them in the operating room, but they always remember the friendly face who took care of them on the ward," he added.

"I tried to do my job, sir."

"And you did it well, son. If you ever change your mind about radiology, there will always be a spot for you in our surgery program."

"Thank you, sir."

"I suppose we never had the opportunity to talk about things outside patient care. Anything you wanna talk about?"

I had a question in mind but I was still intimidated by his presence.

"Come on, son. This is your last opportunity," he encouraged me.

"Sir, I do have a question."

"Fire away, Rastus!" he said, enthusiastically.

"Sir, what does..."

"What does Rastus mean?" he cut in. "I knew you'd ask me."

"Ever since the first day on your service, you've called me Rastus. What does it mean?"

"You really wanna know?"

"If you don't mind."

"It's an old derogatory Southern word, something like a low form of life. Or maybe a simple life. Or maybe a wedge."

"Wedge?"

"A wedge is an old Southern term for a simple tool."

"I see. But what does it have to do with being an intern?"

"An intern, in many ways, is like a simple tool. A tool that is used to get the job done. That was you, Rastus. A simple tool. You don't ask questions. You just do the job. You keep the patients going."

"I see."

"That's how I like to think about my interns. But you were a little different, I must admit. You wanted to question my service. You tried to make sense of things in your own little way. I know that it was hard for you at times. You made it difficult for yourself, especially during the first few weeks. We didn't have a good start together, but eventually you got used to your role. You accepted things better. It's good to question things but not at your level, son. Leave that for later. Your job as the intern was to do as ordered, to keep things flowing. I know that you were judgmental of my decisions a few times. I know that you didn't like some of them, like what happened with Mr. Jacob. But one day, son, you'll understand better. You'll have more experience under your belt." He paused for a while as he contemplated the flowers surrounding the table. "Time is a great teacher, son. Life isn't clear cut. There are many tough decisions one has to make, and if you're a cardiovascular surgeon, you have to make those decisions often. It's no joke, son. It's a matter of life and death. I have to decide for these people. I have to play God, sometimes. Not that I like doing it, but society expects me to. People want to destroy their bodies with cigarettes, fast food, guns, accidents, and then they come to me and expect me to play God. They put their trust in me. They put me in a position of power, a position of control. They come to me with great hopes. They think I'm in control. Isn't that what you think, too?"

"Yes, sir. You're the boss," I replied. "There's no doubt in my mind."

"It seems that way, son. But believe me, I'm not. The patients are the boss. They control my life. Every second of it. I'm the slave of their medical needs," he said with a sad voice. "I'm the poor man shoveling coal into the engine to keep the train running. They're the passengers on the train and they can get on and off as they please. But I'm stuck in the engine room, shoveling pieces of coal. Now think about it, son. All the long days we had together this year. All the times we were stuck in the operating room well into the early morning hours trying to save someone's life. Do you remember the Christmas dinner I missed because of that ischemic foot? How about the weekend trip I had to cancel because of the ruptured aorta? Do you remember the day my wife was about to deliver our premature little boy? Wasn't I in the operating room with Cutter and you?"

"Yes, sir, you were," I answered.

"Son, the patients are the boss and on my service, they always will be. You and I are just the poor men shoveling coal. Keep that in my mind."

"Yes, sir."

"I know you hated my service at times. The sixty-hour stretch you did, the crazy patients and their families, the annoying nurses... I know it was hell for you. It was for me, too. But you have an option because you're off this service the minute you leave this garden. You may have spent a year in hell, but you're walking away from it today," he said, pointing to the entrance of the terrace. "Look at me because I don't have that option. For the next thirty years of my life I'll be dealing with these patients and their problems. I'll be up many nights taking care of their emergencies. I'll be missing holidays, anniversaries, and birthdays because of them. Things are never the way they seem. Just remember, son, I'm just shoveling coal. You're getting off the train, but I'm stuck in its engine room. I have to live with the heat, the dirt, the dust, and the smoke. That terrible smoke will choke me to death one day."

I didn't know if he was expecting me to comment or not. In any case, I didn't know what to say. I listened and thought about every word he said. I realized that after all, he was no better off than me, the intern. And he was right about one thing: I was getting off, but he was to continue the ride.

"I can't leave the Harshberg service because I AM, AND WILL ALWAYS BE, THE HARSHBERG SERVICE!" he exclaimed.

He was indeed the Harshberg service, and if anyone would have asked me at that moment, I would have told them that his service was one of the best in the country. He was technically trained to perform the most difficult cases. His skills were outstanding, but more importantly, he had the wisdom and honesty to advise his patients about what he thought was best for them. He might have made a few mistakes, but he was well intended. Maybe he didn't care much for the patients after the surgery, but at least he was there when they needed it done, and he made sure that their care was not compromised. We, the residents, were his sergeants, the caregivers. He set high standards for us and pushed us to our limits. But he also gave us the independence to care for them and learn from our mistakes.

"I believe I've said what I've been wanting to tell you for a while," Harshberg said, as he got up and covered his head with his hat. "Maybe now you'll understand what this year of your life, called internship, was all about. I wish you luck."

"Thank you, sir," I replied, as I shook his hand.

"By the way, make sure you see my secretary before you leave today. She has something for you."

He turned around and walked away. I stood in the garden and watched him disappear. I was missing his service already, his jokes, his constant harassment, Cutter, and the word Rastus.

"Professor Harshberg left you this," said Mrs. McCleve, his secretary, as she handed me a big box wrapped with gift paper.

"Do you know what's in it?" I asked, curiously.

"No, but I know he has never given a box like it to any of his past interns."

"Thank you, Mrs. McCleve, for your help and support," I said. "And of course, for your patient listening."

"Please do keep in touch. We'll miss you around here."

I carried the box and quickly walked to the parking lot in search of my car. I laid it inside my trunk and wondered about its contents. Finally, I reached for a knife inside my doctor's bag and cut open the box.

Two things were inside: a brown cowboy hat and a small envelope, with a thank-you card. In it, Dr. Harshberg had written with black ink:

To Rastus: I could give you 10,000 reasons that you did a great job on the cardiovascular surgery service! I am envious of you and your future. The sky won't limit you. Just remember to put your clothes back on, unless you want to walk around like that...
Willie Harshberg

His words were in reference to the 10,000 units of heparin which almost cost Mr. Peterson his life, to my promising future in radiology, and to our first meeting with Mr. Merck when we found him sitting on the examining table half-naked!

- Forty-six -

"Are you nervous?" Melodie's mother asked me, as we stood in front of the Memorial Church at Stanford.

"I'm shaking," I replied.

"It's a normal feeling. She's very nervous, too," she said, as she looked at Melodie who stood ten yards away from us. With her mother's Guatemalan wedding dress on, she looked like the love goddess crowned with purple lilies.

"Isn't she beautiful?" I asked her.

"She's my girl and I've been waiting for this day for a long time," she added with teary eyes and a brief hug. "It's sad that her father isn't here to see her. She meant so much to him. I hope, Mick, that you take good care of each other."

"You have my word, Mrs. Fabella. As long as there's life in me, Melodie will only know the sweetness of life."

She smiled happily. "I'm glad she has you. I know how Mediterranean men love," she said, squeezing my hand.

"So what do you think of the church?"

"Gorgeous. Is the mosaic made of gold?"

"It was built in memory of the university founder and his son, by the university co-founder, Mrs. Stanford."

"A true masterpiece," Mrs. Fabella said, as she looked around. "I love the Spanish architecture, the red tiles, and the palm trees. They go so well together."

"What you see was all inspired by love," I commented.

"We're ready for you," the usher announced, as he came out of the church.

"Let's go, Mick. It's your day, today," she said.

The church big wooden doors suddenly opened and the ushers invited us in. Three large organs played the Concerto in D minor by Bach as we slowly went down the aisle surrounded by many of our friends and family, including Dr. Ungaman, Dr. Melstein, Dr. Gastein, Dr. Harshberg, Ron, Inger, Mrs. McCleve, Linda the respiratory therapist and her new Hungarian lover.

Once we reached the altar, Melodie's mother walked to the left front seat and I turned around to face the doors. Father Schnur acknowledged my nervousness by laying his hand on my right shoulder.

Silence reigned for about two minutes as everyone waited with great anticipation. The back door slowly opened again and the shadows of two people emerged as they crossed a tunnel of sunbeams linking the outside of the church to the inside. The organs played Voluntary In E by Stanley as Melodie was led down the aisle by Fred, my barber. I looked at her eyes which reflected the golden walls of the church. Love was pouring from her face. I lifted her left hand and bent forward. I kissed it and kept bowing.

"Dear family and friends, we gather here today to bless and unite together Melodie Fabella and Mick Baldi," the priest said. "On this special day, we ask God to help and guide them in their long journey together. I cannot think of a more memorable moment in life than this moment. In front of you and me, stand two hearts that share one love, one life. With love and joy come responsibility and commitment. The success of any long-term relationship has three elements: an honest and sincere commitment, communication, and a healthy attitude towards life. Marriage isn't an easy journey but it is a rewarding one." He paused and cleared his throat. "On this sacred occasion, I turn to you, Mick, and ask you to honor your commitment, to freely and openly discuss your emotions and thoughts with your Melodie, to be supportive of her efforts in life to pursue her dreams, to encourage her to become what she wants to become, and to ease her fears. And now, Melodie, I speak to you and ask you to love Mick, to comfort him, to be understanding of his commitment to medicine and to helping others, and I ask God to give you the patience and the will to put up with the demanding life of a doctor," the priest said, pausing for a few minutes as the organ playing resumed.

"This Holy Shrine has seen the matrimony of many couples but today is a very special day. It's your day, Melodie, and yours too, Mick. As you stand here in front of me, and before I declare you husband and wife, I must ask each one of you if you're ready to undertake this journey together. If you have doubts, now is the time to speak up. Please, come closer to me."

We took a couple of steps forward.

"Mick Baldi, are you willing to take Melodie Fabella as your beloved wife, to love her, support her, be with her in her brightest and darkest moments, be faithful to her and be with her and only her, forever? If you do, say 'I do'."

"I would be honored, sir," I answered.
"Please answer if you do or do not."
"I do. I do. I do..."
"Once is enough. I think we all heard you," he said with a brief smile. "Now, Melodie Fabella, are you willing to take Mick Baldi as your beloved husband, to love him, support him, be with him in his brightest and darkest moments, be faithful to him and be with him and only him forever? If you do, say I do."
"I do," Melodie said softly, tears flowing down her face.
"Now, I turn to all present here as family and friends and ask you, if you have an objection to this union, please speak now or forever hold your peace." He lifted up his head and looked at the audience. He waited for a few seconds and then faced us again. "Blessed are those who love and honor their commitments. As the priest of this church, I have the privilege and joy to..."
His speech was disrupted by noise coming from the back of the church. Everyone turned around to look. The back doors opened and two shadows entered the church. "Wait. Please wait," everyone heard one of them say.
"A couple arriving a bit late," the priest announced.
"Please wait. Doctor Baldi. Doctor Baldi."
The second I heard the way my name was pronounced, I recognized the voice: Merck had made it to the wedding. He took a few steps forward with the help of his crutches. A young and pretty Asian woman was accompanying him. She had on a short black miniskirt with a white shirt. Merck was dressed in a striped blue and white suit with a flowery bow tie. His right leg was missing.
Standing in the front row with his wife, Harshberg turned around and looked at him. He shook his head a few times and then looked at me. I could read the 'Oh, shit' sign on his face. I saw him whisper in his wife's ear.
"Please, wait. I came a long way. I don't want to miss the kissing part!" Merck exclaimed.
Everyone laughed.
"Who's this man?" the priest asked me.
"He's one of Dr. Harshberg's dearest friends. That's how I met him," I responded.
"What happened to his leg?" he whispered, in my right ear.
"It's a long story, father. But I took it off."

He was shocked by my comment. "Well, if he's Dr. Harshberg's friend, he should sit next to him," Father Schnur added, as he walked down the aisle to meet Merck and his Asian companion. He helped him walk to the front seat and sat him right next to Harshberg.

Then, he walked to the front of the church and faced the audience again. "Blessed are those who love and honor their commitments. As the priest of this church, I have the privilege and joy to unite you as husband and wife. You may kiss the bride now."

"What a great day for the both of you," Harshberg said. "I wish you all the good luck that life can bring."

"Thank you, Dr. Harshberg," I replied.

Melodie wrapped her arms around me as we sat in the back seat of Harshberg's new Explorer. He and his wife sat in the front.

"Rastus, how long have I known you?"

"Almost two years, sir."

"Well, son. I don't want you to be calling me sir or Doctor Harshberg anymore. Just call me Willie."

"Yes, Willie."

"Now, where's that winery we're going to?"

"Napa Valley."

"Finally, I'm going to see Napa," Mrs. Harshberg exclaimed.

"You need to tell me how to get the hell out of this campus. I never thought that this place was so big. What's that thing to the right?" he asked.

"Which thing?"

"The big tower over there."

"Hoover's last erection."

"Hoover's what?"

"Hoover's last erection. That's what the students call it around here. It was erected in the honor of President Hoover who was a Stanford student."

"Quite an erection, I must say!"

"Well, how do we get out of here before Hoover's erection falls on us?"

"Go straight down this road until we reach the highway."

"The inside of the church was so inspiring," Mrs. Harshberg commented, while looking back.

"It felt like I was in heaven with all of those angels painted on all the walls," I said. "Or I must say almost like heaven until little Satan walked in!"

"Who?" Melodie asked.

"He's talking about Merck," Harshberg said. "I never knew that he was coming to your wedding. I thought the guy was still recovering in the nursing home."

"Oh, no. He recovered some time ago. I've been in touch with him in writing. I wanted him to be here."

"I know how much Joe means to you. But I can't believe that I saw him again. And the priest sat him next to me. What is it with him? Am I ever going to be able to get rid of him?"

"I'm afraid that you're stuck with him forever."

"I must admit that he looked pretty good today. I told you, Rastus, I may die before the bastard does!"

"One never knows."

"Yes, son. One never knows."

"I hope that you don't mind, but he'll be sitting at your table up at the winery."

"Joe?"

"Yes. I thought for old time sake."

"Boy, am I looking forward to this. What have I done wrong to deserve sitting with Joe?"

"Now, be polite Willie," his wife warned. "You're a guest just like him."

"I can't wait to see the bastard drunk."

"Willie..." she said.

"And who was that young Asian beauty with him?"

"His wife," I answered.

"His what?"

"His wife."

"You must be joking. Where in the hell did he meet her?"

"After his last hospitalization, he decided to make the best out of his remaining days. He came so close to death. It was a miracle that he survived his cardiac arrest. So after he got to the nursing facility, he contacted the Asian love connection. It's an agency that finds suitable Asian wives for American men. He saw her picture in their catalogue and ordered her right away. They delivered her to his nursing home within two weeks."

"Amazing! How old is she?"

"Twenty-five years old. They were married in the nursing home about six months ago. Since his recovery they've been back in his small town in northern Arizona."

"Joe. Joe. The son of a bitch never ceases to amaze me. He beat the odds and survived six big operations. He went to hell and then decided to come back to this world in the last minute. And now he got himself a young babe. The man is a legend."

"He's a legend, I agree. I don't think that I'll ever forget him."

"What's the name of that agency again?" he asked with a big smile on his face. Mrs. Harshberg hit him on the head. He adjusted his hat. "Just kidding, honey. Just kidding."

"You better be."

"Honey, you know that I love you more than anything else in the world."

Melodie kissed me on the cheek and hugged me stronger. She was thrilled. But most of her excitement was related to the drive with Professor Willie Harshberg, not the wedding. She had heard so much about him.

"What a gorgeous day to celebrate this big event," Harshberg said, as we got on the highway. "I can't wait 'til we get to the winery."

"I bet you can't," Mrs. Harshberg responded. "I know that you want your liquor today."

"You're right. I just can't wait to party with little Joe and have a few drinks with him. I might as well get used to him."

"Now, you be nice to him up at the winery. I don't want any surgeon's talk up there."

"Yes, ma'am," he responded.

"It's nice to see a man listens to his wife," Melodie commented.

"Believe me, honey, he has no choice," Mrs. Harshberg looked back and smiled.

"You just have to listen," Harshberg added. "Wives are like nurses. They can make your life easy or they can make it hell if you piss them off."

"I must say that you learned that early on, Willie."

"Life, what a big tragedy!" he exhaled. "Here, son. Here's to you and Melodie," he continued as he pulled a bottle of Scotch whiskey out of his jacket. He unscrewed the top and took a big sip.

He extended his arm and offered me the bottle. I hesitated for a second and then grabbed it.

"Men! That's what you have to look forward to!" Mrs. Harshberg told Melodie.
"I know. But what would we do without them?" she replied.
"A lot of things. Believe me, a lot of things. I'll be happy to tell you later."
I took a few sips and squeezed the bottle between my legs.
"Where is that bottle, son?"
"Sir, you can't drink and drive?"
"Goddamn it, Rastus. Just call me Willie. Now where's that bottle?"
"Willie..."
"We can't miss out on the fun. The celebration starts now," he replied.
"The cops won't be happy, sir."
"The sons of bitches are never happy anyhow."
"You may get in trouble."
"Trouble? What's life without trouble? Trouble is what life is all about for a cardiovascular surgeon. Give me that bottle, son."
I handed it back to him. He took a few more sips, then looked in his rear view mirror.
"You know what, son?"
"What?"
"SOMETIMES YOU JUST GOT TO SAY WHAT THE FUCK! JUST WHAT THE FUCK!"

And 'what the fuck', is all we said to life as we drove up to Napa Valley while listening to country music just like in the old days of operating room seven. Willie and I got wasted. He ended up in the back seat with me while his wife drove the rest of the way with Melodie next to her. He was no longer the mean and aggressive surgeon who welcomed me in the operating room on day one of internship. He was just another ordinary fellow. He was just Willie.

Many speeches were delivered at the winery. Most of them didn't make much sense. But everyone was drunk and it didn't matter. Everyone laughed and applauded. The food was exceptional. The music played by a band of twenty-four Mexican mariachis made the party an eternally memorable event. Everyone danced under a clear sky full of beautiful and distant stars. I was happy to see all the people who had touched my life before and during internship together celebrating. There were no doctors, no nurses, no patients, no barbers, no priests. There were only common people who tried to forget the world beyond the premises of that small and charming California winery.

And on that night, I was reborn again. Reborn as a man who only wanted to live and die with one woman, Melodie. Reborn as a doctor who only wanted to ease someone's pain.

God bless internship year!

Two years went by and many things changed. On a beautiful, sunny morning, Merck collapsed at the breakfast table struck by a heart attack. He was buried in northern Arizona. Kari had a few more boyfriends, but not a fourth husband. Harshberg changed his attitude towards television surgery and learned how to handle the laprascope from Dr. Schinstein. Last I heard, Cutter continues to climb the surgical hierarchy with his unmatched zeal for cutting.

And I, Mick Baldi, decided that radiology wasn't really for me. Well into my second year of training at Stanford, I quit my position because I missed the operating room, the chaos and the emotional roller coaster ride that surgeons experience every day. As I conclude the last sentence in this book sitting on a plane en-route for an interview at the ACLS, I wonder whether I will be at Harshberg's mercy once again...